Barbara Cleverly was born in .... ⌐ _
graduating from the University of Durham spent most of her
working life in Suffolk and Cambridge, where she now lives.
Her first novel, The Last Kashmiri Rose, *was commissioned*
after she successfully submitted an outline in a competition
for new writers organised by the Crime Writers' Association
and The Sunday Times. Published to great acclaim in 2001,
The Last Kashmiri Rose *was set in India in 1922 and*
introduced World War I veteran and detective hero Joe
Sandilands. It was chosen as a 'Book of the Year' by the
New York Times. Barbara Cleverly's third Joe Sandilands
novel, The Damascened Blade, *won the Crime Writers'*
Association's Historical Dagger in 2004.

Four of the stories included first appeared in the 2013 anthology
'Cambridge Mysteries'

Other titles in Ostara's *Cambridge Crime* series:

R E Swartwout: *The Boat Race Murder*
ISBN 9781906288 006
Aceituna Griffin: *The Punt Murder*
ISBN 9781906288 013
Douglas G Browne: *The May Week Murder*
ISBN 9781906288 020
V C Clinton-Baddeley: *Death's Bright Dart*
ISBN 9781906288 037
V C Clinton-Baddeley: *My Foe Outstretch'd Beneath the Tree*
ISBN 9781906288044
V C Clinton-Baddeley: *To Study a Long Silence*
ISBN 9781906288 198
V C Clinton-Baddeley: *Only a Matter of Time*
ISBN 9781906288 204
V C Clinton-Baddeley: *No Case For the Police*
ISBN 9781906288 211
Christine Poulson: *Murder is Academic*
ISBN 9781906288 396
Michelle Spring: *Nights in White Satin*
ISBN 9781906288 495
T H White: *Darkness at Pemberley*
ISBN 9781906288 532
F J Whaley: Trouble in College
ISBN 9781906288 730
***Q Patrick*:** Murder at Cambridge
ISBN 9781906288747

The New Cambridge Mysteries

Barbara Cleverly

Ostara Publishing

Ostara Publishing 2015

This collection © Barbara Cleverly, 2015

Stories © Barbara Cleverly, 2013* and 2015

[* some stories first appeared in Large Print and Audio versions in 2013]

ISBN 9781909619265

A CIP reference is available from the British Library

Printed and Bound in the United Kingdom

Ostara Publishing
13 King Coel Road
Colchester
CO3 9AG
www.ostarapublishing.co.uk

Contents

Cambridge Past

A Night Climber

Cambridge. June 1922

John Redfyre sprang awake muttering an oath he thought he'd left buried in the mud in northern France along with the rest of four years of filth. Alert, but with an old soldier's stillness, he lay trying to work out what had disturbed his sleep. He'd planned to get up at six and he knew instinctively that he'd not overslept. There - in confirmation, the clock of Peterhouse College across the churchyard cleared its throat, hesitated and launched into its slow and sombre count. Six.

The postman wouldn't call for another hour and this narrow lane between the church of Little St Mary's and the river was always deserted until five minutes before the first lecture of the day. Yet his dog was growling in the meaningful way his owner had learned not to ignore. An intruder? Redfyre listened for a repeat of the bang or the creaking of wood that must have awakened him.

Oh, Lord! Not the bloody Anglo-Saxon invaders again!

He sprang out of bed and thumped downstairs. The same simultaneous occurrence of creaking wood and dog alarm a month ago had thrown up a nightmare scene down below in his living room. Would he ever forget the yellow-grey bones of a skeleton that had begun to shoulder its way up through the ancient floorboards, its upward progress receiving hideous assistance from the jaws of Redfyre's terrier? The dog had been hysterical, torn between duty to repel boarders with the utmost noise and the impulse to get his teeth silently around the unexpected offering of a cache of bones before someone caught him at it.

Redfyre relaxed on seeing that all appeared to be well this morning. No bony fingers were raised in rude salute. The newly-bought Afghan rug was still neatly in place over the repaired boards.

His landlord had been unperturbed when summoned. 'What do you expect in a house thrown up over an Anglo-Saxon graveyard? Not much in the way of foundations here you know.' Mr Barnwell had fixed him with a challenging and superior look. 'Anyway, you're not exactly a Varsity type are you?'

Redfyre's right fist had tightened and his smile had broadened.

Unaware that he was running into danger Barnwell had sailed on: 'Jolly lucky, I'd say, to find *any* accommodation in the centre of town that's not the preserve of the Colleges. Such a fuss! If you're spooked by a few bones, I can always...'

Redfyre cut him short with an officer's curtness. He really didn't want to move. Five minutes walk to his HQ and the town centre, the sight of a Christopher Wren façade from his front doorstep, wonderful scampering for Snapper through the rough meadow land along the river, these advantages outweighed his pride.

'You're going to tell me it's the dry Spring we're having, Barnwell. Or the wet Winter,' he said equably.

Barnwell picked up the appeasement if not the sarcasm. 'Well, yes. That's right. You were in Flanders, I understand? Then you know that bodies *do* rise to the surface. Popping up all the time, they are!'

Redfyre had grinned. 'Pop up? Bodies follow me around, old chap! But I don't expect them to invite themselves for breakfast.'

'Now, we have a choice,' his landlord had rattled on -

not for the first time on this subject, Redfyre suspected, aware that he owned several houses in this part of town. 'Either we can report this find to the University Archaeological Society and your drawing room becomes an official dig site for the whole of the summer, a dozen sweaty students in your kitchen making tea all day, or I send for my builder and take his advice. Advice which I know will be: "Return, fill and ram." In and out in half an hour. Out of sight, out of mind. What do you say, Redfyre?'

Samuel the builder and an Afghan rug had solved his problem.

He found the dog growling behind the front door, teeth ready to sieze any hand that came through the letter box. Redfyre moved him aside with his foot and told him to shut up but the gargling continued. He bent, opened the letter box and peered through, glimpsing a familiar uniform.

'Stand down, Snapper,' he ordered. 'It's one of us.'

The young officer looked uncertainly round the door as it opened.

'Detective Inspector Redfyre, sir?'

'That's me, constable. What's up? Never seen an inspector in his jammies? Occupational hazard. Step inside. Ignore the dog and don't trip over the rug. You're up bright and early.'

'No, sir, I'm left over from last night. Constable Davies. You're needed, sir. In the city centre. The Super sent me to get you.'

'Oh? Someone bombed the Town Hall? About time. Leave it to burn.'

'No. There's been ... or there's *going* to be... an incident, sir. I'm just coming off night duty. Quiet shift considering it's May Week. No hi-jinks on the river. No de-baggings or malarky of that sort. But, on my way back to the station to clock off, I spotted something a bit odd going on at one of the colleges. At Saint Benedict's.'

'There's always something a bit odd going on at St Benedict's,' the inspector commented drily. 'Especially after dark. They don't welcome police intrusion into their little idiosyncrasies and certainly not at this hour. The colleges are all locked up. No, no - unless someone's hung the Master from the flagpole, I don't want to hear about it.'

The constable refused to be discouraged. 'I reported what I'd seen to the Superintendent and he told me to find you and tell you to take charge. You're to get over there straight away and sort it out. Because you're the only one who can do it, he reckons.'

'Me? I'm going nowhere until I've had a cup of tea. Come through to the kitchen.'

Redfyre released the dog into the back garden and settled the constable at the table which was already laid for breakfast with regimental precision. 'Now - tell me what's bothering you, lad.'

'It's Henry VIII again, sir.'

'Eh? Oh... the old bugger in the niche half way up the front of the building! Best Portland stone, carved in the sixteenth century? That Henry?'

'That one. Well, the Night Climbers are out again and they've been having a bit of fun with him. There's some sort of degree ceremony due to start at ten o'clock in the square below. College ordinands processing from - or did the guv'nor say to? - the Senate House, are scheduled to stop off for a pep talk from the Master on the way, right under the gaze of their benefactor - that's King Henry, sir. And there'll be ladies present in the Master's party. The Super doesn't want them scared witless and blaming him for running a lawless town.'

Redfyre groaned. 'Gawd 'elp us! They've stuck another red cod-piece in amongst his draperies! Thrusting through his doublet at a jaunty angle? Cricketer are you, constable? Couldn't you just have lobbed something at it? Not a cobble for choice - a lump of turnip from the market bins works well - it does the job without damaging the stone-work. But there's no need to make a fuss. I know the sort of ladies who attend these ceremonies. Under their fancy hats they keep heads stuffed full of history and art. A classical fig-leaf hides no secrets from them. They've all passed a probing lorgnette over statues of David, Achilles and Zeus. No, constable, they're well acquainted with the outstanding points of the male anatomy. They while away their idle moments writing literary monographs on Holbein and medieval imagery - they're not likely to have a fit of the vapours at the sight of a counterfeit cod-piece.'

'No, sir. But they might be spooked by a real *shotgun*. Aimed straight at them.'

The constable enjoyed the silence that greeted this and went on: 'You know how King Henry stands, sir, hands on hips, sort of swaggering.' He got to his feet and demonstrated. 'Well someone's stuck a gun - genuine item as far as I could make out - under his right arm. Like this.' Another demonstration followed, the officer's truncheon playing the part of shotgun. 'You've got to hand it to those lads!... The Night Climbers.' He repeated his phrase, savouring the romantic sound of it. 'It can't have been easy, mucking about up there on the ledge in the dark, but they've managed to arrange it so the barrel's pointing straight down at the platform where the dignitaries are going to be seated. The old bird's not going to be firing it - course not - but I have to say, sir, that, once you've clocked it, you can't look anywhere else. It gave me quite a turn when I looked up and saw him taking a bead on me. There's something about a gun barrel trained right at you that gives you the collywobbles... Oh, sorry sir...'

The young man's voice trailed away as he remembered

that the inspector had served with the Rifle Brigade during the war. If anyone knew the terrors of coming under fire, one of those free-wheeling sharp-shooters surely did.

'Bloody hell! This is Cambridge, not Cambrai! And a *shotgun* in the hands of that murdering old rogue?' The inspector was trying not to laugh at the grotesque image. 'Now that's too scary to be a joke! You have my serious attention, lad! Let's never forget that Henry was a wicked old devil. Mmm... A sixteenth century crackpot equipped with a twentieth century means of slaughter... Makes you think! We ask ourselves how many wives did he get through? Six was it? And how many of those had their heads chopped off?'

'Two, sir,' Davies was pleased to supply the information. 'Anne Boleyn and Kathryn Howard.'

'Exactly. A *wife*-killer. Someone's making a point. You didn't happen to notice a banner or placard... something of the sort... accompanying the manifestation? Of a "Divorce Not Decapitation... Degrees For Women," nature?'

'No sir. No sign of anything like a feminist protest. Wouldn't expect it. It's a male college. Females aren't admitted and they don't climb anyway.'

'Mmm...' The inspector came to a decision. 'The Superintendent's right. Now, a feather duster or a pogo-stick would have been just high spirits and we could safely leave them up there to rot away with the rest of their flights of fancy but a gun? That looks bad. Lawless. It'll have to come down. No good waiting for the college to react. By the time they've woken up, taken notice, convened a committee to enquire into the matter and put it to a vote, it'll be next Tuesday tea-time. And, in the end, they'll only come up with the decision that the Dean should ring the police and chew our balls off. Again. Fancy doing a bit of overtime Davies? An extra hour? Good man!'

Noting the expression of weary compliance, he added: 'But you'll be needing your breakfast.' He looked more closely at the young man. Gangly, not enough flesh on his bones. A face intelligent but strained by fatigue. 'Kettle's boiled. Make yourself useful. Four spoons of Assam in the brown pot. I'll get the frying pan on the hob and we'll have a bacon buttie. King Henry can, for once, be kept waiting. Cut the bread will you, while I have a splash about in the bathroom and choose a suitable outfit to disarm the old geezer.'

* * *

The inspector's appearance down below in the kitchen twenty minutes later was surprising enough to make the constable splutter into his mug of tea. He knew what his mother would have said: 'Fine figure of a man!' A bit disconcerting though. He wasn't entirely comfortable with the idea of being seen walking the streets in the inspector's company dressed like that. Still, this was Cambridge in May Week. You came across all sorts. Eastern potentates in full regalia, gesticulating actors in tights and rusting chain mail, swarms of men in ermine and scarlet silk. You soon learned not to look twice. And, of course, at this unearthly hour, there'd be a rush of rowing crews and their coaches, heading for the river in singlets and long-johns. With a bit of luck, the inspector might pass for a sportsman of some extreme kind.

Redfyre stood tall and handsome in an open-necked, black and white striped rugby shirt, white cricket flannels restrained at the ankles by bicycle clips and black gym shoes. He was sporting a pair of racing glasses round his neck and he carried a length of climbing rope slung, bandolier-style, around his shoulders. He was ready for any challenge: the Eiger, The English Channel, the Scottish Rugby Team.

14

'I decided against the tailored Harris tweed and the nailed boots,' he said cheerfully. 'Saving them for the Matterhorn. Will I do?'

To Davies' embarrassment, he struck a swaggering pose, chin up, hand on hip, like a man advertising golfing knickers.

'Very nice, sir. Very sporting,' Davies muttered.

'Right then. We'll carry our breakfast with us. I'll just check the bacon's crunchy and we'll put it between slices of bread and pop it into a couple of brown paper bags. Would you like an egg in there or would that be too squishy? Good. I'll have one too. We'll eat them as we go. Nobody about to see us.'

*   *   *

Redfyre dropped his dog off with the lady down the lane who did his housework for him and the two officers marched up a deserted Trumpington Street and into King's Parade where they ducked down a cobbled street leading to the imposing façade of St Benedict's College. Two Tudor monarchs were holding court over the paved enclosure below: King Henry VIII in the niche on the left and his daughter, Queen Elizabeth, on the right.

The inspector surveyed them both with his glasses. 'Well, the queen is armed, befittingly, with a sceptre. His Majesty, more dashingly, brandishes, not an ordinary "shotgun", constable, but the rather more appropriate Holland & Holland "Royal". It's a big game rifle,' he said, wondering. 'Powerful enough to stop a charging rhinoceros! Question is - at whom is the gun aimed?'

'Come now, sir! Surely you mean - at whom is the *joke* aimed?' The smooth voice came from behind. Redfyre lowered his glasses and turned to confront the newcomer, noting: late twenties, impish good looks somewhat marred by a night on the tiles, evening dress, a distinct odour of brandy. Just the kind of interference Redfyre could do without.

'Good morning. Excuse my lack of top hat. I had it knocked off by a frisky Metropolitan police officer last night in Piccadilly. Or do I mean earlier this morning?' the gent chirrupped in great good humour. 'The Roberts up in London town are not so indulgent with roistering gentlemen as our home-grown Cambridge bobbies. A moment please while I pay off the cabby...'

He fished about in his pocket, and a theatre programme dropped to the ground. *You, too, Eustace*, the musical comedy of the summer in London. Redfyre smiled as he picked it up and handed it back.

'I say - you couldn't lend me sixpence for the tip, could you? Thank you, my man. Much obliged!'

As the taxi drew away to return to the station, Redfyre introduced himself to the stranger: 'Detective Inspector Redfyre and Constable Davies, Cambridge Police. How do you do, sir?'

'Indeed? Well, being the only member of the college about the place, it falls to me to welcome you to St Benedict's. I'm a fellow here. Guy Gifford, History.'

The young don took the glasses from the inspector with a murmured: 'May I?' and peered up at the building. 'Good Lord! What a cheek! The Master will *not* be pleased! I mean - that's his own gun, if I'm not mistaken. His pride and joy. A lavish present from a visting Maharaja before the war. I don't believe he's ever used it, though he polishes the walnut stock himself quite regularly.'

Gifford handed back the glasses and traced the line of fire downwards with a finger. He shot off to the place he'd marked, stood and faced the barrels.

Very steady on his pins, the inspector reckoned, for someone who had avowedly spent the night 'roistering'.

'Ah! I see the joke! Come and look! This is exactly the

16

spot where the Master will be standing later this morning with an entourage of dignitaries and such members of his family as can be persuaded to keep him company. His wife, Lady Tapstone, and their daughter, Allegra... possibly his ancient mother-in law...' Gifford's wicked smile widened as he imagined the scene. 'My, the shrieking and the swooning! Let's hope they have smelling salts to hand.'

'The Master's mother-in-law?' The inspector's alarm was evident. 'She must be getting on a bit? Poor old girl! Let's hope she's not got a dicky heart.'

Gifford turned on him abruptly. 'Now, how the hell....?' He recovered himself and continued: 'As a matter of fact, she is indeed – ancient. Over ninety, I believe. And – yes – she is known to have a dicky heart. But don't be carried away by your compulsion to detect, Detective. This *is* May Week. Japes, hilarity, drunkenness and mischief everywhere you turn.'

'Mischief? Yes... as you say... And trickery's not just the preserve of Academe!' the inspector muttered to his constable with a sly smile. He whispered a few words to Davies who moved off with a grin and a nod towards the arched doorway below the statues, leaving the two men to stare in speculation at the monarch.

And it was rumoured that the old lady had, as well as an interesting heart condition, a tidy fortune to dispose of, Redfyre recalled. He dismissed the thought as unworthy though instantly reclassified it as possibly relevant. Aloud, he commented: 'Always hard to predict how the fair sex will react when threatened with a gun.'

A loud report rang out, shattering the stillness and, in an uncontrollable reaction, Gifford threw himself to the ground, lunging sideways out of the target area as he dropped, bringing the inspector crashing down underneath him.

A horrified constable was beside them in seconds, hauling them to their feet, the tattered remains of an exploded paper bag in his right hand.

'Thank you for the demonstration, Constable,' Redfyre said, chuckling.

'Well! That makes me look every kind of a fool,' Gifford said, dusting off his knees. 'Not much evidence of British *sang froid* in that little performance! I say - I'm most frightfully sorry for the rugby tackle, Inspector.'

'What *was* in evidence was a still finely-tuned infantry-man's reaction to an explosion,' Redfyre said. 'Much obliged! You saved me from death by paper bag.'

'Oh, once a Guardsman... Don't take it personally - I was just using you as cover,' said Gifford with a dismissive grin. 'That was a very convincing noise, Constable! Redfyre, I see you were ahead of me. You've demonstrated that if, at some stage in the proceedings, a loud report were to ring out - a shot from a concealed weapon - up on the roof perhaps - a humble fire-work or even a blown-up bag... heart-stopping emotions might be stirred in those below standing in target range?'

'Indeed. Panic and palpitations might well ensue. Are you expecting to be on the platform yourself, Mr Gifford?' he asked.

'No. I shall be dead to the world by then. Flat out sleeping off the effects of a strenuous night. I was just about to climb back in to the college using a favourite but secret way the undergraduates normally use to avoid paying gate money or getting into bad odour with the Proctor. I shall have to bid you good day and ask you to look the other way while I do this. Sure you understand...'

He began to edge away.

'Wait! A moment, sir. Am I to assume from your remarks that you're some sort of a climber yourself?'

'I climb. I was an undergraduate here before the war. I know the ins and outs. And the dangers: loose guttering, revolving spikes, wobbly pinnacles. It's a death trap up there if you don't know what you're about.'

Redfyre took a deep breath. 'How do you fancy breaking in by a different route this morning? I'm going up to get that gun down and take a look around. The constable doesn't climb and I could do with back up. Especially back up that knows where the toe holds are.'

Gifford stared upwards at the façade, assessing the challenge. 'Anything to save the ladies an unnecessary flutter,' he drawled. Then, fixing the inspector with a flash of mischief: 'You're on! Let's have at it! But had you thought, the joker may be still concealed up there waiting for his moment? We should expect company.'

Redfyre turned to the constable. 'Watch our backs, lad. If I'm not here to relieve you in half an hour, go round to the front and gain entry. Over the porter if you can't get round him.'

He hung the glasses carefully out of the way inside his shirt and rubbed his hands together in anticipation. 'Right then! Let's get a look at it. South face... that's good.' He addressed his remarks to the constable. 'It's the reverse of climbing a mountain, you see, Davies: sunny side good on a building, bad on a mountain. There it leads to avalanches and erosion. Whereas it's on the northern face of a bit of architecture that you get crumbling and decay.'

The constable nodded in pretended understanding, sensing that his governor was just establishing his climbing credentials for the varsity bloke.

Then the don had a go. 'No need for chimneying thank God! I wouldn't want to ruin this suit – I borrowed it from a chum. Lead pipes - do you see - square but not abutting the stone work. We can get our fingers behind. What do you say to scrambling up it as far as that projecting ledge? A few yards of traverse, skirt around the oriel window...'

'Ah, yes. The oriel. The window with the grandstand view of the proceedings. Who's behind those closed curtains, I wonder? Any chance...?'

'No one will disturb us. This is a much climbed façade. Level three of difficulty. Occasionally the faint-hearted will tap on the window to beg entry. The long-suffering bloke who has those rooms gets accustomed to scratchings in the night and people traipsing through. Like Piccadilly Circus some nights, he complains.' He paused and added thoughtfully: 'The present incumbent is a climber himself. And, as you see, well placed to be the perpetrator - or at least a witness - of this piece of nonsense.'

'I shall have a quiet word with the gentleman,' Redfyre promised.

'After that, it's a choice of hand-holds over the stone carving... a plethora of curlicues,' the don supplied with relish.

'One of us, the leader - may I suggest: you, sir - gets up and throws a leg over the apex of the roof... right there... and sits firm, lending a steadying hand and the rope I brought with me for the second - me - to lean out, check and remove the gun. I'll fasten my rope to it and we can haul it up. When we reach a safe place, we can lower it to the ground inside the college.'

The two men exchanged military nods followed at once by self-deprecatory grins and went into action.

The constable watched with envy as they moved with strength and grace, attacking the face of the Tudor building. Backs arched outwards, they swarmed up like caterpillars, pushing and pulling on the pipe with hands and feet. Each set of metal stays they encountered punctuated and boosted their progress upwards. Davies hardly dared to watch their acrobatics over the curlicues. The constable enjoyed a scramble up a tree or down a drainpipe as much as the next lad but he'd never have embarked on a joint enterprise with a complete stranger. And a dissolute toff reeking of brandy? Not on your nelly!

He only breathed easily again once Gifford had safely put his leg over the roof ridge. In moments the two men had brought the rope into play, one end secured by Gifford and the other carefully attached to the inspector who leaned out at a back-breaking angle to extract the rifle from the clutch of the stone arm. Definitely a two man operation this, Davies concluded. He was very relieved not to be the second man.

He was about to wave his trophy in triumph when, seized by a sudden thought, the inspector braced himself, broke the gun and peered into it.

From below, Davies heard the snort of surprise and the string of trench oaths that followed. Redfyre was fiddling with the mechanism. Could he be...? Yes, he was. Davies knew enough about firearms to interpret the gesture. The bloody gun was loaded!

* * *

Gifford was pale with excitement when Redfyre joined him on the roof ridge. 'Loaded? Real ammo? Your man was actually planning to fire it off at someone? Nonsense! Couldn't possibly have worked!... Could it?'

'I wonder... I've made it safe. It was firmly fixed in place with two door wedges which I now have in my pocket along with both cartridges.' The inspector passed him a length of strong cord. 'This was tied around the trigger.' His voice was tight with disbelief. 'We're to assume that someone who needed to keep his head down - over there probably...' Redfyre pointed to a spot some yards off '... intended to lie in wait out of sight of the party below and then tug on this cord which he'd run round that pinnacle, hoping to let off a bullet into the crowd. He? They? Let's keep our eyes peeled for any sign of occupation up here. No! It's a barmy idea! Would never work.'

'All the same - would you offer yourself as target to test

out the theory, Inspector? Not sure I would. To think we were prancing around down there, peering up into an elephant gun with two up the spout and some maniac's finger attached to the trigger!' Gifford shuddered.

'If we're to assume malice aforethought - and I do - it's been carefully staged,' the inspector suggested. 'There's something deeply sinister about this piece of theatre. Anyone going to this amount of trouble to position the gun must have rehearsed somewhere quiet with the cord, calculating angles and tugging-power required.' He added heavily: 'Well, well! Death averted this time - let's hang on to that - but I shall have to follow where this cord leads. I'm afraid I need to investigate further. At worst, this could have been a case of premeditated murder or random slaughter. Unsuccessful and quite mad but who's to say something similar won't be attempted again? And more carefully thought out next time?'

They set off along the roof, jumping down into a trough where they paused to take in the architectural jumble of copings, ledges, parapets and connecting walls around them.

'This is his HQ or his redoubt, you might say. Have a good look around, Gifford.'

Gifford grinned. 'You mean he might have conveniently left a monogrammed cuff-link or a banker's letter for us to find? Fat chance!'

Redfyre leaned over the parapet and stared down into a grassed courtyard below. 'Ah! We can do better than that! He's left himself!' With a strangled exclamation, he leaned farther out and Gifford grabbed him by the belt with a warning cry.

'Look! There he is! There's our prankster!' Redfyre said in a voice chilled by horror. 'Still at the scene. But I'd say he was not enjoying his joke.' Redfyre grunted. 'Death averted, was I saying? Huh! It would seem it's ghastly old

Death who's had the last laugh.'

* * *

The internal descent was easy and brought them all too quickly to the body lying slumped on its front on the grass. Black plimsols, socks, tweed plus-fours and a black sweater were as might be expected: the usual discreet attire of a Night Climber. He was lying face down, a snug woollen climbing hat pulled down around his ears. Redfyre approached, a silent Gifford following on. The inspector held out a hand to deter his companion from rushing forward. When he was satisfied he had absorbed the information he was seeking from the damp grass on which the figure had landed, the inspector at last stepped close and gently pulled off the hat.

Redfyre gasped, Gifford gave a rasping choke and leapt back in alarm as a shining bob of fair hair, released from the constricting wool, sprang into sudden and alarming life and blossomed like a chrysanthemum around the head.

'A girl, by God!'

Redfyre was aware of Gifford exclaiming and muttering in the background but the body claimed his attention. He checked for signs of life and finding that she had been dead for some time, he tried to ascertain the cause of her death. The head was lying at an unusual angle.

'Neck broken in the fall,' he concluded. 'No sign of damage to the body otherwise.' He looked up, assessing the height from which she must have fallen. 'It wouldn't have been impossible to survive such a drop. The landing on this grass is soft enough... damp with dew... and the soil below is sticky with worm-casts. She must have landed awkwardly. What bad luck.'

He began to examine the limbs that were exposed, paying particular attention to the wrists. He looked at the woolly hat he still held in his hand and frowned.

Gifford finally spoke in a hushed voice. 'But it may not have been bad luck, Inspector. She may have thrown herself from that height deliberately. They say suicides dive down head first to be sure, don't they?'

Redfyre freed her features from the curtain of hair, looking with pity at the blue eyes, open wide in terror.

'Poor child,' he murmured. 'If she had meant to do it, she regretted it at the last. I'm wondering why, if she intended to kill herself, she would go to the trouble of fixing up the paraphernalia of the gun? Was she a killer or a suicide? I don't think she could have been both.'

'One followed by the other?' said Gifford. 'Not unknown.'

Rolling the body over, Redfyre's attention was caught by an edge of white fabric. He tugged it free. A length cut from a bedsheet had been turned into a banner on which was painted in red letters: *Degrees For Daughters!*

'She was about to make a statement, then. Could she have been working with a partner? Job like this takes two. A disagreement broke out up there on the roof top?' Redfyre speculated. The inspector looked again at the hat. 'Or did something altogether more sinister occur?'

He looked sharply at the silent, stricken figure of his companion. 'Time you told me what you know, I think, Gifford.'

'Yes. Of course. I didn't think I'd fooled you. My first thought was: suicide. You ought to know that she'd been threatening something of the kind for the past few weeks. And this is the very place she would have chosen.' Gifford pointed an unsteady finger at the windows of a graceful Georgian insert into the older fabric of the college. 'Directly opposite, do you see, inspector? Those south-facing windows? The breakfast room of the Master's lodge. When Sir Thomas comes down for breakfast and stands there, greeting the day with a chorus of the Eton Boating Song and doing his deep-breathing exercises, as is his annoying routine, he'll catch sight of her body.'

'Are you going to tell me who this is, Gifford?'

'It's Allegra Tapstone. The Master's daughter. And, as you will soon discover – my cousin.'

* * *

Redfyre knew he ought at this point to have made a formal announcement of some sort. Issued a warning. Taken the man into custody pending interrogation. Not for the first time, he ignored the rule book and followed his instinct. A camaraderie develops quickly between two men sharing a climbing experience, however short their acquaintance. He sensed that some vestige of this trust lingered between them, a slender thread that would not bear much weight. Certainly not the weight of handcuffs. And, had he imagined a look of uncertainty, a half-spoken word, a slight feeling that the man wished to confide something to him?

He bent and gently closed the girl's eyelids.

'A lovely young woman,' he murmured. 'God save her soul.' And, after a pause: 'You were her cousin, Gifford, but were you also her friend?'

He'd found the right formula apparently. Gifford's upper-class stiffness melted, the cockiness drained from his voice, leaving a young man's stumbling uncertainty. 'Yes! At least I tried to be... Ally is four years younger than I am and has no brother to look to. I have no brothers or sisters either, so we were close as children.' He took the girl's cold hand in his. 'I used to help her to her feet when she fell over as a little thing. She was very roly-poly... always tumbling down.' His face contorted in a spasm of grief and he swiped at his eyes with his sleeve, looking aside to hide his emotion, until he was able to go on. 'Four years of study and four years of war cut us off from each other of course and we'd both changed fundamentally by the time I came to lecture here. But we remained, I like to feel, friends, in spite of everything.' He stopped abruptly, thinking he'd said too much.

'Do you know who her other friends are? Have you any idea who her accomplice might be? I doubt she could have undertaken this prank by herself.'

'You'll be asking her father that question of course. She was friendly - over-friendly some considered - with one or two of the undergraduates. In a hush-hush sort of way.'

'Undergrads? Bit young to be of interest to her, surely? She must be... mid-twenties?'

'Twenty-six. Hardly a girl, though as you see, with her delicate frame and elfin looks, one would have guessed - nineteen. There are all sorts and ages of men here, after the war years, picking up their interrupted studies, their interrupted lives. Most are in search of a lost world of tea and crumpets and high moral values.' His ironic tone and sour look suggested he was not one of these. 'Some are seeking the means to destroy that cosy world and reshape it. Old? Young? It doesn't matter any more. You're either the late-lamented or the glad-to-be-still-alive, now.'

Thoughtfully staring at the lifeless face he went on quietly and quickly, flicking a glance at the Master's window every few seconds. 'I'll be frank. Ally was a bold young lady, if you take my meaning. "Emancipated" she would have said. Suffragette of course. She did war work in London. Not quite sure what but her parents disapproved. She got in with a fast crowd at the Admiralty. And when she came back home she was still looking for adventure. But perhaps her thrills were not of a fleshly nature, Inspector. Perhaps that was no more than her parents' nasty suspicion? She could have been involved with nothing more improper than a Night Climbing Club. It could have been as innocent as that... An exhilarating climb under the moon with like-minded companions... an illicit drag on a Woodbine up there amongst the chimney pots... I never believed she was as wicked as her father makes out.'

Redfyre caught the icy tone. 'Strained familial relations, are you implying?'

'No need to talk like a policeman! The old bugger tortured and tormented her all her life. She was not the son he wanted. Nor yet the dutiful daughter who would just about have been acceptable. Her mother is a weed. A drooping, broken woman whose fortune the Master has enjoyed and exhausted but whose company he despises. She is far from being a comfort to her daughter - she is a whining, resentful presence.

'Allegra's father made a mistake he is not even aware of having made in the rearing of his daughter. He hired a Scottish nanny for the rejected child the moment she was born, an intelligent and loving woman in whose care she blossomed. And then he compounded his mistake by sending her away to school. Allegra was educated at a no-nonsense establishment with a forward-looking headmistress who made her the girl she is. She emerged spirited, clever, physically and mentally able to run rings around her own parents. She ran away from home when she was eighteen. The first year of the war.'

'Why did she return here?' Redfyre quickly answered his own question: 'Of course, she must be financially dependent on her family...'

'You're right. Her maternal grandmother it was who insisted. She is the lady who holds the purse strings in this family. Disliking her own children - and who shall blame her? - the old girl skipped a generation and made Allegra and me the two main beneficiaries of her will. She made it a condition of inheritance that Allegra toed the line and gave up her London life. She's been desperately unhappy ever since. If she's taken her own life, I hold her monstrous father and her manipulative grandmother responsible for my cousin's death. She chose her spot deliberately, inspector.'

'Would you care to explain that?'

'She could never command her father's attention while she was alive. I think she was trying to penetrate his indifference by this demonstration of death right before his window.' Redfyre didn't quite like to see the gleam in Gifford's eye as he added bitterly: 'At the very least, she planned to put him off his porridge. I think we should help her, don't you? I owe her that much. Don't queer my pitch, inspector when I confront him.'

The young don was speaking angrily but spontaneously. No thumbscrews required here. Redfyre listened, nodding his understanding as he hurried on. 'Look, old man, it's about time for my uncle's appearance in the breakfast room. When we've alerted him to his loss, if you don't mind, I'll make myself scarce. I might well lose my temper and enter another death on your slate. I'll be in my room if you want to see me again. Any of the college servants will bring you to me - staircase C, number 5. And here comes your constable to join us, right on time, running ten yards ahead of the under-porter!'

Suddenly the blind at the window of the Master's lodge shot up.

* * *

The startled expression on the shining morning face was clear even across the courtyard. Through the glass the Master signalled his objection to the presence of an uninvited audience for his morning chorus and the three men instinctively gathered themselves together in a group and waited for him to approach.

Sir Thomas Tapstone stepped out through a french window and came on towards them over the grass with all the confidence of a man heading a procession. As soon as he was within earshot he began: 'Well, well! What do I find here? The insalubrious residue of a night's carousing? The fag end of a fancy dress party? Who've we got? Maurice, the Mayfair Masher? Percy Plod, the Plebeian Policeman? And... and...' Even this self-assured toff was having difficulty categorising the inspector, Davies noted with satisfaction. 'Mr Bassett, the Liquorice Allsort? Or is the gentleman in the form-fitting striped ensemble trying for Captain Webb, the Channel Swimmer?'

This heavy sarcasm was embarrassing enough but the wretched man had caught a glimpse of the body they'd been trying to shield from him. 'And - ha! - behind you there's a fourth, if I'm not mistaken. Louting about on the lawn! Collapsed in a state of inebriation or vomitation...' He pointed to the recumbent form of his daughter. 'Stay close Herbert,' he told the porter, 'I may have to ask you to take this lot in charge for trespass.'

Redfyre recoiled at the mis-placed humour. He disliked the accompanying sneer, the false bonhomie, the air of unquestioned authority. The man's spruce appearance, from his shining bald scalp to his polished toe-caps was intimidating. He held back and allowed Guy Gifford to respond.

'Uncle! Good morning! May I present Detective Inspector Redfyre, and Constable Davies of the Cambridge Constabulary who are here investigating a case of some concern and behind us...' He stepped aside with a conjurer's flourish, '...you see the cause of that concern. Not "louting about on the lawn" but lying dead in the dew of a broken neck, is your daughter, Allegra.'

Redfyre winced.

'No! Are you mad? What is this charade? Get up at once, Allegra! No one is amused!" shouted the Master, his composure shattered. He made no attempt to approach the body but stared at it, his jaw working, bulbous eyes alarmingly distended.

Redfyre's sober tones filled the silence that followed with police formulae of confirmation and sympathy, his attention fixed on the Master's every changing facial expression as the man took in the enormity of the situation facing him.

'She fell off the roof in the night? That's what you're telling me? How many times did I warn her against... nay, *forbid* her to set foot up there? You will bear me witness on that Guy! But an accident. Following on a student jape. No need for the police to stick their noses in. And I'm sure I needn't remind you that discretion in such unfortunate cases is of the essence...' He sighed and consulted his pocket watch. 'Today of all days! The Lord High Sherrif and his lady wife are due to join us for the ceremony in three hours. Three hours! I must ask you to vacate the premises, inspector. At once!'

Redfyre flashed a warning look at Gifford who showed every sign of exploding into a physical demonstration of his rage and began to speak, his voice taking on a chilly drawl. 'I don't much care, Sir Thomas, if you're parading the Chancellor himself, preceded by three Esquire Bedells with maces reversed. My work here will take as long as necessary. You may count on a heavy police presence in your college for at least the rest of the day and thereafter until such time as I deem the case to be solved. You may, accordingly, wish to take instant steps to cancel the ceremony or, at the very least, divert it away from the college precincts. And perhaps you would care to confide to me your plans for conveying the news of her daughter's death to your wife?'

Tapstone swelled with indignation and spluttered angrily: 'The deuce I will! What sort of bobby takes it upon himself to dictate practice and etiquette to a college principal who has just viewed the body of his daughter killed in a regrettable accident? I don't care for your attitude. I suggest, my man, that you leave directly. By the tradesman's door. The porter will escort you. Herbert! The policeman is leaving.'

Gifford, who had listened with a wry smile to this exchange, intervened. 'Uncle, I think you were not attending when I gave the gentleman's name.' He repeated: 'This is Inspector John Redfyre, M.A. D.S.O. C.I.D. You know you really ought to read the newspapers. The inspector is a graduate of Trinity College and is in possession of a better degree than mine - or yours. He is also a much decorated Rifleman. He does not use the tradesmen's entrance.'

Tapstone gaped and his eyes narrowed as he looked more closely at the inspector. 'Good lord! Yes, I have heard you spoken of. My apologies, er, Redfyre. At least they've sent their best man.'

Before his uncle could commit further gaffes, Gifford interrupted. 'Aunt Grace takes breakfast in her room. Look - I'll volunteer to go up and break the news if anyone thinks that a good idea.'

'A moment, Gifford,' said Redfyre. 'I'll do that myself. You may go up to your own rooms now but I must ask you to stay there. Constable Davies - remain on guard right here. When I return, you will commandeer a bicycle and go at once to HQ. Tell the Super to send out support. I'm setting up a Scene of Crime operation.'

He turned back to the Master. 'We are not dealing with an accidental death, Sir Thomas. Nor yet a self-inflicted one. Your daughter has been murdered.'

*　*　*

The Master gasped and his head rocked back as though he'd received a blow to the jaw. He recovered to say without bluster: 'You can't be sure of that!'

'I am. And we shall shortly have the medical evidence to confirm.'

31

Tapstone's eyes narrowed in calculation as he focussed on the retreating figure of Gifford. 'A death which leaves that cousin of hers with a clear field... Lucky young Guy! Potentially a very rich man...' He recovered and continued in dismissive tone: 'Well, well. Fickle, purblind Fate deals us some strange hands, inspector, as you are well placed to know. We are all at the mercy of the goddess Fortuna.'

'Oh, I don't know, sir. I'm not a great believer in Fate. I've always thought Milton made a fair point when it came to free will: ... *what I will is Fate.* I'm with Satan on that one. Necessity and Chance have little to do with it.'

'Indeed. Milton has much to teach us. But it is my duty to direct the investigation towards the man who killed my daughter. You'll find him in Room 6 of Staircase A.'

The master pointed to the ancient part of the building they had just climbed.

'Would that, by any chance, be the room with the oriel window overlooking the square?'

'It would. And the gentleman's name is Edward Hazzard. Post-graduate, pacifist, free-thinker and thorn-in-the-flesh. He and Allegra were as thick as thieves. I was on the point of sending him down. Oh, and Eddie Hazzard, if you twist his arm, will probably confess to being Allegra's lover.'

Eddie Hazzard was sleeping peacefully in a tangle of bedsheets when the porter opened up his room. He didn't wake as Redfyre walked to the window to assess the view over the ceremonial space below but when the inspector tapped on the glass, the reaction was instant wakefulness. Yawns were punctuated by curses and exhortations to 'Get lost, whoever you are! Put a bloody sock in it! How many more times? Where the hell did I...?' He groped about on his bedside table and grabbed at the pair of glasses Redfyre helpfully held out for him. He peered through the thick lenses at the policeman and asked:

'Who or what the hell are *you*?'

Redfyre picked up a ragged teddy-bear from the floor and, with an emotion he didn't quite like to identify, he handed it to the young man. 'Put your dressing gown on, lad, I'm afraid I have some very bad news,' he said gently.

* * *

In the St. Andrew's Street headquarters, Superintendent MacFarlane of the Cambridge C.I.D. heard his officer Redfyre's end-of-day report delivered across the width of his mahogany desk with mixed feelings. MacFarlane was an able man, well-endowed with intelligence and common sense and had risen through the ranks at the slow pre-war pace. While part of him admired his younger officer's confidence when it came to taking on the upper classes, he shuddered with foreboding at his boldness and assumption of authority. 'One day that lofty manner of yours will get you into trouble I can't extricate you from, my boy!' he'd often said and it seemed at last that day had come. His comments as Redfyre's tale unfolded were littered with exclamations of: 'You never!... Tell me you didn't say that!... For God's sake, Redfyre, that's both our jobs gone for a Burton! Even *your* connections won't save you now!'

But his eagerness for the chase soon reasserted itself. 'So - you've got him down in the cells, this Hazzard bird? I'll go and take a look at him.'

'No, sir. I've made no arrest yet. I thought I'd wait and get *you* to sign the warrant when we're certain.'

'Sounds ominous! I'm taking no steps until we have our facts copper-bottomed. These are influential people and damned clever. They have the County Commander on a string. Anything less than a confession of guilt, signed in blood, on college writing paper, won't swing it.' He gave a smile of evil anticipation. 'So - what are we

33

waiting for? Let's get one! Are you going to tell me who you have in your sights?'

'Not yet.' The inspector grinned. 'I've no objection to arresting a toff but it had better be the *right* toff! At the moment we've got a merry-go-round of three chaps each blaming the one in front. Gifford fingers the Master, the Master declares Hazzard did it and Hazzard's got ten bob on Gifford.'

'Running a book, are they?'

'I came near to quoting them odds! Everyone involved has a strong fancy – apart from Lady Tapstone.' He shuddered. 'Awful ten minutes, that was, sir! Breaking the news - never easy, but this woman is weird. Controlled. Thanked me politely for letting her know... Was sure the matter was in good hands... Didn't seem at all surprised. So Allegra had got herself murdered, had she? One of the girl's naughty tricks... Always in a spot of bother! Had her father been informed? Serve him right for not asserting his authority. Not as though he hadn't been warned... End of conversation.'

'Dignified but deranged, eh? At least she didn't go for you with a hatpin like that she-wolf I had to deal with in Newnham College!' The superintendent twitched. The old wound still troubled him. 'Now, what's next?'

'One or two further bits of evidence to come in. Response to a call I made to the Bow Street nick and a report from the grandmother's lawyers. But, not least, I want the post mortem examination results. I gave instruction for that to be given priority.'

'Quite right, my boy. Ring them up again. Use my phone.'

He listened as Redfyre was connected with the police medical unit.

'First things first, doctor... No sign of earth from impact on the top of the hat she was wearing I noticed. You can confirm?... And both wrists intact which would be inconsistent with a fall - even suicides instinctively put out their hands to ward off final impact.' He repeated the encouraging phrases for the super's benefit, waggling his eyebrows in triumph. 'And you're saying: fracture of neck bones suggests *strangulation*, not a fall from a height... Ha! Thought as much. Frontal grip apparent from thumb impressions on neck. So we can say she was killed right there where her body was found in the courtyard? Yes... Though there were flakes of stone in her clothing, consistent with climbing having been done. Mmm... Death occurring between three and four o' clock this morning.'

His eyes gleamed as he replaced the receiver in its cradle. 'The autopsy is still in progress, sir. That's all they'll let me screw out of them.'

'Lawyers even more tight-lipped,' MacFarlane grumbled, passing over an envelope. He summarised as the inspector read. 'They take a whole page to say it's none of our business. But - sod them! - always a good idea to follow the money, Redfyre.'

'If we do that, we come face to face with the one remaining heir - as we understand it at present. Gifford! The one bloke who was sixty miles away at the time of the murder. Just climbing aboard the first train of the day at the estimated time of death.'

'Mmm... he gets in just after six, and half an hour later he's at the scene assisting the police to effect an entry into the college. That's quite an alibi!'

'I know that train,' Redfyre admitted. 'Leaves King's Cross at four, wanders all over south Cambridgeshire picking up milk churns and disgorges a motley company of exhausted gents a good mile and a half from their colleges.'

'You've checked...?'

'Of course. I'd noted the number of the cab. The driver was a good witness. Remembered Gifford clearly. He picked up our bird with a crowd of others when the London train came in. They dropped three off to climb into King's and Gifford came on to St Benedict's by himself. Paid the whole fare. Cabby never wants to hear a chorus of "*Eu, Eu, Eustace, it's you!*" ever again.'

'Pity. What else have we got? Nothing but an avalanche of emotion... Just where we don't want to be! Family problems, hatreds and jealousies, spurned lover... Ugh! This teddy-bear fancier, Hazzard, you seem to be going so easy on? Socialist troublemaker, by all accounts. The Red with the Ted in the Bed - he's on our books. I fancy him for the job. Why aren't you so keen, inspector?'

'I interviewed him as he was coming out of a deep sleep. A sleep following on a disturbed night. Is it possible to murder your lover and fall instantly asleep? Shouldn't think so. I don't think you can fake that. And I don't think he could have cobbled together such a load of codswallop if he'd been guilty, sir. It was the middle of the night when the first scratching came. The usual coded noises asking for entry. He got out and opened up, grumbling. Two climbers came in, giggling and slapping each other on the back. He wasn't listening with much attention but was left with the impression they were up to some monkey-business of a May Week flavour. He didn't check identity - that's just not done. It's a very secretive association. He went back to bed again. A further entry was requested later that night by a solitary climber who did at least identify himself and apologise for the disturbance. A first year beginner who lost his nerve. And, lastly, he was woken by the sound of a police petard below in the square.'

'A what?'

'Fart, sir. Davies' performance on the paper-bag.'

MacFarlane sighed. 'Climber himself, we understand, this Hazzard?'

'So Gifford said. But, strange thing - the chap's as blind as a bat. He couldn't see me until he'd put on his specs.

Admits to having done some climbing in his first year but for the last two years his eyesight's been failing. I don't think he'd get far up a drainpipe. Odd that the Master should have pointed me towards him with such certainty?'

'But he had a particular relationship with the dead girl?'

'They shared a political view. Were members of the same societies. Not hard to guess he was pretty much in love with her. But affection unrequited. Older woman, a rich one potentially. Way out of his orbit, he suggested.'

'And Hazzard fancies Gifford for the job, did you say?'

'From certain curses he uttered in his grief of the: "So the fiend did for her at last..." kind, yes, that's what I understood. Not a reasoned response, sir. It was just a cry of protest torn from the heart.'

'Hearts!' the superintendent said tetchily. 'Can't be doing with 'em! Pockets – now you know where you are with a pocket. Get on to that lawyer again. Poke a stick at him.'

'He'll have to wait until I get back from the station tomorrow morning,' Redfyre said mysteriously.

* * *

At the sound of the early train approaching, Redfyre nipped into the station by a side goods delivery gate, armed with the platform ticket he'd bought a minute before. He strode out past the ticket collector, waved through with a gaggle of weary travellers. He reached the taxi rank a short head in front of a group he'd selected and jovially invited the men to share his taxi into town. His new-found friends dropped off at various points in the city and the inspector got out himself at police headquarters. He was holding in his hand a programme of last night's performance of Beethoven's Seventh at the Albert Hall, tweaked from the pocket of one of his fellow passengers.

'Easy-peasy,' he told the superintendent. 'He could have done it.'

'Ha! And there was a message from London, Bow Street, this morning. No top hats confiscated. No altercations in Piccadilly at the time in question. Got him!'

'Got him for *something*, at any rate,' Redfyre said doubtfully.

'Everything! He was the girl's partner. They fix up the gun and deliberately show themselves to Hazzard who witnesses a *pair* of conspirators. A joke or something more sinister? We'd better ask. They climb down. Gifford strangles her right there in the courtyard and then belts off to his room to change into evening gear and pop a hip flask of brandy into his pocket. He sneaks out, walks to the station and performs as you did just now. How am I doing?'

'On facts, perfectly, sir. Not sure about motive. I mean why would they go to all this trouble?'

'Alibi. Jokery and climbing - that's a sending down offence if you get caught. They'd want to avoid being suspected. The nonsense with the gun was a two man job, clearly. Allegra being a woman, her name would not come to mind. Unless seen in connection with another strong suspect: Gifford. So - eliminate *him* from the possibilities. If he hadn't spotted bluebottles swarming round his little scene, he'd have got out of the taxi at the front gate and made a fuss. He wanted to be noticed. He'd have paid a gate fine, cursed the porter - memorably - and had the time logged.'

'Rather a good prank and I'm sure he's the perpetrator but why spoil the joke by killing her?'

MacFarlane groaned. 'Oh, come on! You bust a gut setting up the alibi - you might as well do the crime! Pity to waste all that effort on hiding a student prank. He throttles her and hopes it will be assumed she died in a fall. He also throws in the suggestion of suicide to further distract the forces of law and order. And it would have worked if I hadn't had the forethought to send in a lynx-eyed, bolshie copper with a posh voice to catch 'em out. Any other representative of the Plod would have been escorted to the kitchen to get a cup of tea and a slice of fruit cake and sent packing. They would have hauled in some family doctor to sign the death certificate and she'd have been six foot under right sharp. And Gifford is now his granny's sole heir. Hmm... I think we're ready. Hand me that warrant and I'll fill in his name.'

'No. Not yet,' Redfyre held on to the warrant, not fully understanding his reluctance to hand Gifford over to the full force of the Law. There flashed into his mind the engaging grin the man had beamed at him from his perch at the apex of the roof; he remembered the reassurance of the young man's strength and skill on the other end of the rope that connected them and Redfyre squirmed with discomfort. He didn't want the next rope he saw to be knotted in a hangman's noose around Gifford's neck. 'I need more time. I haven't even gained access to the girl's room yet. I must take a look. You never know... Girls keep diaries.'

MacFarlane snorted at his indecision but conceded: 'You're right, lad. Leave no page unturned. Off you go! And take the warrant with you. Just in case.'

* * *

The room was clean, neat and ready for inspection. There was very little of the girl herself in this space, Redfyre reckoned. He noted the bag packed and left behind the door. A diary, open invitingly on her desk, was a college one, listing lectures and official dates. Allegra Tapstone had fled.

'You'll find nothing here.' The remembered voice came from the doorway. 'This is not where she lived her life. I saw you come up. I thought you might like to have these.' Gifford handed the inspector a pile of notebooks and letters. 'She kept her private things with me in my quarters. I've always hidden her secrets for her... broken dolls, rude books, letters from boyfriends... the bottom layer in my sock drawer for years.' He smiled. 'I think you've worked it out, haven't you?'

'A trip to the station coinciding with the arrival of the King's Cross train helped. And the lack of a top hat on the trophies shelf at Bow Street confirmed my suspicions,' Redfyre said agreeably. 'All circumstantial evidence though and we can't book you for it as I'm sure you calculated. A possibility, not the certainty I'm looking for.'

'And you're here to get that certainty. I'd better come clean.' Gifford hesitated, his confidence evaporating.

'The charade with the gun was just that? Miss Tapstone was planning to shoot it off and make her escape over the rooftops just before the party arrived, I'm assuming?'

'Yes. No serious harm intended, inspector. We didn't really expect it to work. Though if the old granny had obliged by keeling over with the shock, there would have been relief all round. Ally had reached breaking point. She was planning to run away again and she wanted to go out with a bang. She hated the college and its attitude to women; she hated her father and wanted to ruin his day. Possibly his career. You can imagine what the press would have made of the episode! He'd never have lived it down.'

'And why were you so ready to help her?'

'It's what I do... did. Cover for her. I love her. Always have. We were planning to get married, inspector, but this would not have been viewed favourably by the old moneybags. Grandmother is not mad - she has always been a vicious, life-denying, manipulative woman. She enjoyed tormenting her daughter and son-in-law by

40

going over their heads and willing the cash to me and Allegra. But further - she played the pair of us off against each other. "Do as I say and leave London, my girl, or your cousin inherits," and: "Resign your commission, Guy - I will not risk leaving the family fortune to a soldier. Oblige me in this or Allegra shall have it...."

'Well, Allegra had had enough. She'd decided to find employment in London. I was going to join her when the dust had settled. This is a family that abuses and consumes its young, inspector. We had decided to cut the ties, break the mould, shake the kaleidoscope. Fashion our own world.'

Gifford fixed the inspector with a steady eye. 'I had to dash for the station. A long walk. I left her where you found her when I went off to change. She said she was going to celebrate her last night in what she saw as a book-lined cage spending a quiet moment puffing defiantly on a cigarette and glaring at her father's window. She'd prepared the banner you found in her pocket to display as a last protest. Her way of saying goodbye. But, inspector, I'm aware you have evidence that I was the last person to see her alive and that I have the strongest motive for doing away with her. I'm assuming you're here to arrest me.'

Redfyre nodded.

'If you do, the case will take its course right to the gallows.'

'That is so.'

'Has it occurred to you that what you have on your hands, in that case, is not one murder but *two* and the second is one which you are yourself working strenuously to bring about? My death, inspector.'

'As you say. Tell me, Gifford - what testamentary arrangements has your grandmother made should you also disappear from the scene?'

The young man frowned and considered the problem.

41

'It never occurred to me to wonder. One hardly expects to die before one's granny. I would guess that she would be reduced to leaving her goodies to her sole remaining relative – her own daughter, Allegra's mother.'

'And Sir Thomas would have his hands on his wife's fortune in minutes?'

'Just so.'

'Two more questions, Gifford. Was Sir Thomas in the habit of walking the grounds at that hour of the morning? And, if so, would his wife be aware of his movements? Did he share a bedroom with Lady Tapstone?'

'Not for many a year. She has a rather grand apartment all to herself on the first floor, overlooking the courtyard. So, no, she would not have been aware of any nocturnal ramblings. And, yes, he often walked abroad in a proprietorial, swaggering way. To smoke the cigar he was not allowed to smoke indoors, to compose his lines of bad verse, to catch the night watchman sleeping at his post... that sort of thing. Also, on occasion, he ventured out when summoned by a porter to attend his wife. A lady of nervous disposition, you have probably concluded. Insomnia, hysteria, depressive characteristics... mad as a bat, in short. She won't last five minutes after she inherits before he shoves her into an asylum under lock and key. Her doctors, whom he pays well, will doubtless have no qualms about committing her and can, indeed, do so with a clear conscience. Two signatures is all it will take.'

'And he will have undisputed access to all her worldly goods according to the law of the land.'

The two men looked at each other with dawning horror.

'We must act quickly! Wives may not testify against their husbands but she may be prepared to help us if she can be alerted to her predicament. I'm going up to call on her, Gifford. And this time I'd like you to accompany me. I may need back-up.'

* * *

Sinisterly, the voice that told them to enter was that of the Master himself.

Redfyre recoiled from the disturbing stink of heightened emotion in the air. Energy unleashed by a bitter exchange between the man and wife snarling at each other across the room was still perceptible. He hurried to wrest the sharp letter-opener from Grace Tapstone's hand and position himself between the two.

'Take him away, inspector, before he kills me!' she panted. She clutched her heart and pointed an accusing finger. 'Goodness knows, he's been trying for years! I should have spoken out. But - how could I? He and that doctor of his have been subduing me with their pills and potions. Between them, they've turned my brain to tapioca.'

Sir Thomas flopped onto a sofa, mopping his forehead and sighing with relief. 'Don't listen to her nonsense, inspector. No need to concern yourself - I'm making no charges. Grace is not herself today, you'll find. She's not thinking straight. If you'll excuse me, I'll go and call her doctor.'

'Stay where you are.'

'I *am* thinking straight!' Grace insisted. Her eyes gleamed, she radiated energy. 'I stopped swallowing your poisons two weeks ago. And you hadn't even noticed, such is your husbandly concern! I poured your laudanum down the sink. I began to find myself again - the woman I used to be.'

The Master's face turned grey and he swallowed. 'Grace, my dear, there are some things better left concealed...'

She turned a pleading face to Redfyre, seeking his understanding. 'I mean the woman I used to be before the child... that horrible, screeching infant who ruined my life...'

43

'Never got over the birth, sad to say,' Tapstone hurried to explain. 'Difficult... Complications, don't you know... Heavy medication became necessary I'm afraid. Right from the start. Ask the doc.'

'There was a moment of clarity. Two nights ago. I couldn't sleep. I stood at my window enjoying the moonlight on the roof tops for the first time in years. An uplifting sensory experience – like bursting out from a fog. But the idyllic scene was blighted by a movement in the courtyard below. Two climbers. One of them took off her hat the better to indulge in a fond farewell kiss with her paramour and I saw that it was my daughter Allegra. I'd know that ridiculous flue-brush haircut anywhere. Disgusting, immoral girl! She proceeded to light a cigarette and then she set about unfurling a banner... *Degrees for Daughters* or some such rubbish! Selfish, selfish child! Why does she expect to have everything? A degree, a profession, a lover? A fortune? Why should *she* have Mama's money? The fortune that should be mine? Why should anyone suppose I am content to moulder away within these walls, walking always in the shadow of that appalling, boring little man?'

Redfyre's voice was chill with dread as he asked: 'What did you do, Lady Tapstone?'

'I went down to the courtyard and demanded that she account for herself. Her usual bravado and self-absorption blinded her to the change... the strengthening... of her mother's character. She was defiant. Taunting me. She boasted about her intention to fire on the degree party and then run away, leaving us a laughing-stock. I couldn't let her go on bringing her family into disgrace. In my new-found clarity I knew exactly what I had to do.'

She held out her hands to the inspector in a gesture worthy of Sarah Bernhardt playing the part of Lady

Macbeth, that other Mother from Hell. 'Strong thumbs, you see. And she has such a little neck. I should have been allowed to strangle her at birth. You were quite wrong to stop me you know, Thomas. You see where your weakness has led us?' With a disconcerting change of mood, she directed a bracing smile at Redfyre. 'Come now! No need for that sad face, inspector. Sympathy and understanding were always wasted on Allegra. She was a fallen woman. She had found her level in the gutter playing with other guttersnipes.'

The Master was the first to break the silence. A dry croak, a hissing sigh and then, barely audible: 'I cannot find the words. The diagnosis, inspector, is best left to the poet I believe you admire:

Demoniac frenzy, moping melancholy
And moon-struck madness.

That is what we have to deal with. The madness of the full moon. It's what I have been struggling with all my married life and I'm weary of it. The subterfuge, the denials, the constant anxiety. The expense. The violence. What do you propose? We are in your hands.'

Redfyre shook his head. 'The same chap also said: *Yet I shall temper Justice with Mercy.* I shall have to take your wife away, sir. The Law requires it. But I shall do my best to ensure she receives both the justice and the mercy she denied her daughter.'

The inspector walked home down the lane at the end of the day, wrung out by the clashing elements of emotional strain and tedious report writing, affected more than his professional self wished to admit by the swirling affairs of a turbulent family. He picked up Snapper from his housekeeper's cottage and hugged the little dog all the way home. He unlocked his own front door and threw the dog in. 'Any bones lying around, you're welcome to them, old chap!' he said. 'I shan't have the strength to stop you. Time, I think, to take my landlord's advice again. Out of sight, out of mind. Return, fill and ram. Pull a rug over it. There'll be a fresh problem tomorrow.'

The Cantaber Common Horror

Cambridge, June 1922.

Clara Croft squealed in sudden shock. She dropped her dishcloth into the sink and leapt back from the kitchen window.

'Did you see that, Mrs Taylor?' Clara appealed to the cook who was counting out spoons of ground coffee into a pot.

'Four... five... Did I see what, dear? Six... he likes it strong.'

'Something at the window... a face... Someone's got into the back yard.'

Mrs Taylor sighed and tutted in irritation. 'They've forgotten to bolt the side gate again! But who would be coming round to the tradesmen's entrance after dark?'

'A Peeping Tom?'

'Huh! He'll be disappointed then! Who's he expecting to see - the Queen o' Sheba? Cook and kitchen maid in full uniform is all he'll get! Not much to peep at!' she said comfortably. 'It's these big windows. And these electric lights. They draw the eye. With them on, any passing 'erbert expects a three-reel picture show!'

'Could be one of them gypsies off the Common. Fair's on, don't forget.'

'Nah! They all upped sticks and left day before yesterday. They don't hang about. There's nothing out there now but wilderness, rubbish and herds of cows.'

Clara glanced at the black expanse beyond the window

and shuddered with distaste. Smart modern house this might be with indoor conveniences, French range and fridge the size of the Mauretania but she missed the crowded warmth of the central city court where she'd grown up. Paradise Court. Crowded with washing lines and handcarts and bikes and always a queue for the communal lavvy at the end, it had a name which could only be wishful thinking or outright sarcasm but it was home and Clara Croft missed the security and closeness of her family and old mates. All that was a half hour's walk away now and she was only allowed a visit to her parents on Sundays.

'That weren't a cow I saw.'

'It'll be the moon then. It's a full one tonight, they say. It looks bigger out here in the back of beyond. Better close the curtains though. Just in case.'

Sensing her young companion's unwillingness to move back to the sink, Mrs Taylor made an effort to bump her out of her paralysis. 'Go on, Clara, love - move! It wouldn't be right for the two of us to be throwing temptation at poor souls, would it?' She gave a comic waggle of her generous breasts, a gesture that would normally have raised a shout of scandalised laughter from young Clara. But whatever Clara had glimpsed in the back yard had snuffed out her good humour.

The girl turned warily back to the window and reached up to pull the curtain across. She screamed again and recoiled, shuddering and gabbling.

'There *is* someone there! But it's not human!'

'Whatever do you mean, gel? Either it's human or it's not. Can't be both!'

'It's white. A face. Staring eyes. Huge mouth. It shot across the top of the window... up there...' she pointed. 'Leering down at me! Like it knew me, Mrs T.' And, pulling herself together: 'Shall I ring for the butler? Mr Anderson ought to come and have a look.'

'What? In the middle of a dinner party? He wouldn't be best pleased.' Mrs Taylor glanced at the clock. 'He'll have just cleared the crème brûlée and got the savoury on the go. Next up: the port. "Be ready with the coffee early, Ida," he said, "and serve a dish of rose and violet creams with it for the ladies. Sweeten 'em up a bit!" The ladies don't get on. The gentlemen won't be lingering over the port tonight if they've any sense. It's tricky timing for Mr. Anderson. If you fetch him down here with stories of a boggart in the back yard, he'll give us both a wigging. And check the level he's marked on the cooking sherry.'

Mrs Taylor thought for a moment then said carefully: 'Clara - you wouldn't have...? You haven't by any chance... attracted a *follower* have you?'

'A follower? Me? Gerraway! The Missus wouldn't put up with *that*! If I had a gentleman friend she'd chuck me out on my posterior in five minutes. No, course I haven't!' Clara's big blue eyes - too big and too blue for her own good, Mrs Taylor reckoned, registered affront at the question.

'Right. Well, if you say so...' Mrs Taylor frowned and wondered whether she could believe her. Clara's pretty face was indignant but she was a lively girl and attracted some attention in the locality with her open manner and easy smile. 'How about next door's new footman? That young bloke at Number 3 who fancies you? He came reeling home drunk the other night and wandered down the wrong snicket. Mr Anderson had to deal with him. Happen he's gone astray again!'

'No, Mrs Taylor. Not after a dealing-with from Mr Anderson! He's the *old* footman now. Been dismissed. He's not around any more. Annie at Number 2 says he was right miffed when he got the boot.'

Suddenly Mrs Taylor began to laugh. 'Got it! Those kids the other side of the gardens came back from the fair the other day with a bunch of balloons! They were painting faces on them and scaring each other silly all afternoon. Noisy little blighters! That'll be it. It's an escaped balloon bobbing about out there.'

The two women relaxed, agreed, and began to giggle.

'Go on out and see to it,' said the cook. 'I'm getting behind with this coffee tray.'

'Can I take your rolling pin, just in case?'

'Help yourself, dear. Leave the door open if you're nervous!'

Clara, suitably armed, opened the kitchen door. She peered out into the back area and beyond to the wild common land heavy with the scent of May blossom. She paused, breathing in the chill fresh air, then grinned and, playfully hefting the rolling pin to her shoulder like a rifle, she stepped outside with a mocking burst of a soldier's song. Mrs Taylor smiled to hear:

'Goodbye-ee, goodbye-ee
Wipe the tear, Ida dear, from your ey-ee...'

A moment later Clara called back: 'All's well, Mrs T! Boggart's buggered off!'

'Language, Clara!' Ida Taylor yelled back automatically.

'While I'm out here I'll just check the garden door *is* bolted.'

Ida heard the girl's steps across the yard and a smothered oath as she banged her toe on a coal hopper. There was a moment of silence and then Clara called back: 'Yer, that's all right. Bolted up good and tight. Returning to base!'

Mrs Taylor next heard the clunk of the rolling pin falling to the paving stones and a piercing scream. A sound like a rushing wind and a flash of light fixed Ida to the spot. 'Gawd 'elp us! Clara! Get inside!' And, with memory of the recent war still fresh: 'It's them Zeppelins back again! Dropping bombs on us!' she shouted. Recovering the use of her limbs, she ran to the door.

She fell back as Clara reeled in past her, her hands

50

covering her eyes, mewing with pain and terror and collapsed onto the floor.

'I've rung *twice* for the coffee! What, may I ask, is going on down here?' The butler, Scottish, authoritative, strode into the kitchen. Anderson stopped and sniffed the air. 'And what's that awful stench? Have you let the milk boil over again?'

He followed the direction of Mrs Taylor's pointing finger and staring eyes and dashed over, falling to his knees beside the girl. Capable ex-batman's hands went to work checking for signs of life at neck and wrist. 'Ida! What the hell have you done?'

'Tweren't me, Colin! There's a Zeppelin out there... or a boggart...'

Anderson knelt by the twitching girl, listening as Mrs Taylor's tumbling account washed over him.

'Jug of water, Ida! Quick! The lassie's still alight! Someone's tried to set her on fire! Stop flapping, woman, and pour it over her head... That's right... Ach! The stink! Her cap's still smouldering. Pull it away, can you? Try not to bring the skin off with it. Any ice left? There's some in the champagne bucket. Just the job. Fetch it over.'

'Is she a gonner, Mr Anderson?'

'She's still alive but she's not with us. And I doubt she'll ever get those eyes open again. If she survives.'

He looked up in sudden horror. 'By God, Ida! I know what this is! *Flammenwerfer!*' He spat the word out with hatred. 'I've seen sights like this staggering back from the trenches. And smelled 'em! Hooge 1915, it was. Burning flesh and hair... you never forget it. There's some mad bugger out there mucking about with a flame-thrower. We'd better send for a doctor.'

He looked up and added lugubriously: '*And* the police! You don't aim one of those infernal machines at someone for fun. He wanted her dead, poor bairn, whoever was out

51

there. We're looking at attempted murder, Mrs T. At the very least.'

'Murder?' whispered Mrs Taylor. 'Murder, in Cantaber Terrace?' Struck by a further paralysing thought, she murmured: 'And police? Colin, unless I'm much mistaken... aren't they already with us?'

*　*　*

Superintendent MacFarlane twinkled agreeably at his inspector over the width of his shining desk.

'Now, tell me Redfyre - how do you get along with wimmin?'

John Redfyre frowned. He could guess where this was leading. The Super had three ways of referring to the female sex. They were: ladies, women and wimmin. Another assignment to raid one of the brothels in Fitzgibbon Street coming up, then. He'd only just recovered from the last disastrous foray into the Cambridge underworld. A black eye and a dislocated shoulder had earned him the respect due to an officer who leads his squad of uniformed P.C.s from the front but the incessant flow of rude jokes that followed behind his back was beginning to annoy.

'Women, sir? In much the same way as I get along with men. I always try to make myself agreeable. If that doesn't work, I shoot 'em.'

'Don't arse about, Inspector. From a man with your war record, that comment could be construed as alarming.' The Super remembered that this inspector was immune to flattery or reproof and reverted to his usual brisk brevity. 'I'm about to hand you a new case. It has come to the attention of the Chief Constable of the County - did you get that, Redfyre? - it has aroused his personal concern and interest. Murderous attacks are occurring and it is feared - on a serial basis.

52

'The victims are a very particular group and precisely located. So precisely, the next victim can tell you her name if you go and ask. That is if she has not already given in her notice and gone home to her mother.'

Redfyre groaned. 'Rosie Hawkes' Pleasure Palace again, sir? Pick someone else. She'd see my grinning face at the door and blacken the other eye.'

The Superintendent pursed his lips to bite back a quip and commented: 'Odd that. They knew you were coming, you know. Not a male client in sight and the girls were barricaded in and armed. And you bore the brunt of it. I'm surprised you haven't made further enquiries in that direction but that can wait for another day. Your talents are wasted mucking about with vice. This here's a proper case for you to get your teeth into.

'No, I'm sending you to a more salubrious part of town. Though it does involve wimmin. You will have to talk to them. Listen to their stories and filter out truth from a slurry of gossip and speculation. Charm them a bit. It's the New Policing. I'm referring to the almost exclusively female staff employed in the rather grand terrace of houses that runs along one side of Cantaber Common. The newly built one. Kitchen maids, cooks, housekeepers...'

At last he had triggered Redfyre's interest. He caught the full blast of the officer's sharp grey eyes and stopped in mid-sentence.

'I know the ones! Interesting architecture. I've watched it going up. Slightly overblown and uncomfortably uncertain in style. Whose style? Lutyens-esque? Voysey-ish? Have you visited, sir?'

'Er... no. Seen 'em from a distance. Some people like them. A few can afford them. They're selling fast, I'm told. Cambridge is expanding outside its medieval boundaries. Trades and manufactories are moving in and their owners need somewhere to live.'

'No use looking in the centre - it's all owned by the university.'

'Exactly. He handed Redfyre a file. 'Here's what we have. The notes made by the squad of uniformed men who investigated at the time.'

Redfyre read the title stuck on the front cover with a smile and a raised eyebrow. 'The "Cantaber Common Horror" sir? Sounds like something you'd stage at the Arts Theatre for a short run in the week before Christmas.'

'It's not a joke. Someone is setting fire to kitchen maids, one after the other. We could equally call it: "The Unexplained Assaults on Maidservants by Person or Persons Unknown, Commencing on the 1st of June in Cantaber Terrace, Cambridge."'

'Very well, sir. "Horror" it is then.'

'Right. Before we go any further - where do you stand on the supernatural, Redfyre?'

'Could my view possibly be of interest?'

'Come on! Don't be shy! You know what I mean. Ghosties and ghoolies and long-leggety beasties.'

'They don't exist.'

'That all you have to say?'

'To a sceptic, they don't seem worth a discussion. Fireside stories from a distant past, invented to account for events and fear that were at the time of first telling unaccountable.'

'Exactly that. Couldn't agree more. But - the *Devil*, inspector? Different kettle of fish, perhaps? I refer of course to the gent with horns, forked tail, scaly red skin and possibly claws.'

This conversation was straying beyond the bounds of eccentricity.

'Ah! That Devil. Yes, I spotted him arm in arm with Queen Cleopatra and Nell Gwyn. Entering the marquee on King's Lawn a fortnight ago. Fancy dress costumiers seem sadly lacking in originality these days.'

The superintendent glowered and waited for a decent answer.

'But devilry, sir? Yes, that exists. I've come face to face with it in humans. Too often.'

'Well, it's rearing its head and snorting fire in a douce Cambridge suburb. The victims - young girls - four of them so far, answered a summons to the back door after dark and received a blast of his fiery breath in their faces.'

'I'm sorry to hear that, sir. But mystified.'

Superintendent MacFarlane passed a sheet of newsprint over the desk. 'I intercepted this at the time of the events.'

Redfyre cringed at the headline: *Horror Stalks Cambridge. Fire-breathing Devil Terrorising Exclusive Terrace.*

'*Cambridge Evening News* - you'll recognise the style. I stopped publication. Called in a favour and uttered threats and menaces. But I can't muzzle the editor much longer if we're caught out by another... er... event. Action required. Reputations at stake. Now listen: the first victim and the most seriously injured was a Miss Clara Croft, kitchen maid at the big house at the southern end. Number 1. The biggest and best reserved for the developer himself, of course. Other domestic staff reported similar unpleasant experiences. Some have given in their notice. Good staff are hard to come by these days and there's, shall we say, a certain amount of dissatisfaction being expressed by the residents regarding the efficiency of the forces of law and order.' He leaned across and confided: 'Ginger being applied to the rear end of the CID.'

'And that's where you find me, sir?'

'Exactly. I want to close this file by the weekend with a felon in manacles, preferably not Lucifer. A credible solution to offer the public wouldn't be bad. There's panic brewing. For reasons you'll discover, they're calling this devilish apparition *Spring-Heeled Jack.* Just so long as he doesn't evolve into a 'Jack' of a different nature! I want no ripping on my patch.'

'Spring-Heeled Jack? After the bogeyman in English folk stories? Do we have a consistent description of the suspect?'

'Oh, yes. Give me that file back for a moment.'

He found his place and began to read in a formal copper's voice: *Spring-Heeled Jack. Apparition reputed to haunt many of the villages in the south and east of England. Enters gentlemen's gardens for the purposes of alarming the inmates of the house.*

'*Gentlemen*'s gardens you'll note, Redfyre.'

'Are we to assume Jack is making some socialist comment on the property-owning classes?'

'Hardly that! No. I was reading from an account in the *Times* on the 9th of January 1838.... nearly a century ago. No socialists about to bother us in those days. But I keep an open mind. Now, it gets more dramatic... Reading from an entry in the *Daily Mirror,* just last year, concerning an attack in Hampstead: *The creature was a cloaked man, eight feet tall, with an enormous head, white face and eyes that gleamed like coals. When he opened his mouth, blue flames leapt out.*'

'*Five local men answering the description were detained but later released,*' Redfyre added.

The superintendent stared.

'Cloaked, sir? Who would be wearing a cloak these days?'

'Some Champagne Charlie off to the opera? Well that *was* Hampstead!'

'Or a policeman, of course.'

MacFarlane went on, grimly, gathering his papers together to show the interview was coming to an end: 'We all know how violence escalates. The first four victims have all survived. The fifth may suffer more than a singed face. Takes a devil to catch one is the theory I'm working on. Look - you may prefer to work under cover. Use your ingenuity. The force are not, apparently, held in high esteem by the domestics up there. The sergeant in charge was physically threatened by one of the old girls. They'll clam up if they get a whiff of police about you. See me back here tomorrow at the same time with his name. By the end of the week at the latest. Don't concern yourself too much with regulations. The Chief is prepared to look the other way for a fast result.'

* * *

Redfyre took the file back to his own office and read it carefully, jotting dates and names in his notebook, suspicion mounting. The first officers had arrived with surprising speed at the scene of the first attack. He wrote a reminder to ask why. Local uniforms in the charge of a sergeant? These boys had, Redfyre guessed, not taken events at all seriously. No one dead, robbed or in hospital. Just the complaints of four servant-girls, that was all they had to deal with. No glory in pursuing that. Clearly a case of female hysteria. One of the coppers had actually noted that the moon was at the full on the night of the first episode. Male shorthand if ever he saw it! And the file had been shelved. Until, after the fourth complaint and the interest of the Chief had been roused it had landed on the Super's desk.

Was Redfyre the only person to see the underlying anomaly in this? Once spotted it stuck out a mile. In all the cases of attacks on women happening in series as the boss feared, the violence built up. Tentative at first, the efforts grew bolder, the perpetrator began wounding and killing with increasing frenzy. Everyone knew that.

In the case of the Cantaber Common Horror, it was the *first* attack that was the most serious, the second a day later, less so, the third, reported two days after that, was muddled and unconvincing to say the least. The fourth, he judged, was a clear invention. All the wrong way around.

Redfyre got out his Ordnance Survey map of the town and studied it. Not much help. The Terrace buildings were too recent to appear on the pre-war edition he had. He pencilled in the spot he thought it probably occupied.

Out in the country, right on the edge of the open common. Fifty acres of rough grazing land, used by cows and occasionally sheep for most of the year but at the end of May the animals were cleared off for the famous Cantaber Fair. A left-over from medieval times, it offered local crafts and produce as well as a small circus with swings and roundabouts for the children. He wondered how the inhabitants of the smart modern terrace managed to put up with the noise. Short lived, however, as the fair moved on after five days. It had packed up and gone two days before the first attack.

Covering as much ground as he could before setting out into the field, Redfyre rang up the editor of the local newspaper and asked him a few questions he had no trouble in answering.

Ronnie Reid was a sharp bloke and he was putting two and two together as Redfyre talked. Half way through reading out dates from his diary the editor fell silent. Then, thoughtfully: 'Oh! Ah! Let's have a look at the programme, shall we? What delights and excitements did they have on offer this year? ... Turkish wrestling... Horse-taming... French Can-can, adults only... Oooo... Well, bless my soul! We've missed a trick there all right, haven't we? We were asked to shelve this story... I say...' A promise of further and better particulars ensured his continuing silence. For the time being.

Redfyre chose to walk the two miles to the outskirts of town. Dressed in white flannels, a dark blue blazer and a straw hat, he looked like any other gentleman about Cambridge taking the air. He took his time ambling about the half-completed terrace of a dozen houses designed to emulate the grandeur of The Royal Crescent in Bath. Numbers one to six appeared to be already finished and occupied. The first was spick and span, a freshly painted and attractive house embellished with an already impressive front garden. The plants were, for the most part, mature and brought in at considerable expense from a nursery. Window boxes were ablaze with geraniums, phlox scented the air beneath the floor-to-ceiling windows. The second house was coming along nicely and so on down the terrace. By the time he reached number seven he had arrived at an unfinished house in a churned-up building site. He poked the mortar in the few courses of bricks that had been erected on the last house and decided no work had been done on it for some weeks. Number eight was still a hole in the ground.

He rapped on the tradesmen's entrance of the house where the fourth complainant worked. He doffed his hat and smiled when a girl of about fourteen peered around the door.

'Beth? Would you be Beth? May I come in?' He took an unthreatening step back and gave her his widest grin. 'I'll tell you straight - I'm a policeman. A detective who's come to hear your story. And I hear you have a stirring tale to tell! Please fetch your housekeeper or cook to listen in if you'd like to. I say - you wouldn't have a cup of tea on the go, would you, love? I'm parched.'

The easy smile, the honest grey eyes, the smart outfit and charming manners opened all doors, Redfyre was disconcerted to find as he worked his way along the terrace. Beth and the cook at number five were eager to share their opinions with him. Beth had had enough. No wounds thank goodness but she was perfectly certain she'd caught him in the back yard. That Spring-Heeled

Jack they were all talking about. She'd told her mum and her mum had insisted she gave in her notice. She was working out the week and she'd be off. And Gwenda next door at number four had done the same.

At all the houses he heard the same story, the same ready and consistent answers to his questions.

The third girl on his list working backwards, Annie at Number 2, proved to be the special friend of Clara Croft and to have genuinely encountered something nasty in the back yard, the evening following Clara's experience. Again a tall locked gate and enclosed garden had apparently been no obstacle to the white-faced, fire-breathing Spring-Heeled Jack she described.

Taking off her maid's bonnet, Annie bent her head and showed a patch of singed hair just beginning to regrow. She'd never forget the stink and the sharp pain as he blasted her with flames! Enjoying Redfyre's sympathy, Annie proved a willing gossip. She was inclined to blame the footman, Alfred, for the prank, though she couldn't for the life of her see how he could have done it. Ladies man! And nasty with it, if the gentleman knew what she meant? He'd tried it on with all the girls in the row. They'd got together and complained to their employers. Alfred had been sent off with a month's severance pay by old Mr Fanshawe at number three who was too generous for his own good. And they were all relieved, except perhaps for Clara Croft, Annie added with best-friend waspishness. *She*'d had a bit of a swing-round with him, though it had all turned sour.

But - hadn't anyone noticed? It had all started after Alfred was dismissed. It was Annie's opinion that he'd come back to be revenged on them for losing his post.

Redfyre spoke next to Clara Croft herself. In response to his show of concern, she proudly showed off her injuries. Redfyre winced in sympathy when she showed him a red scorch mark across her forehead, eyes still swollen and oozing and a loss of hair more extensive than Annie's. The cook and the kitchen maid welcomed him in, eager to tell their tale to a receptive ear.

As Redfyre prepared to leave, Clara summed up: 'I were blinded for a day! If it hadn't been for Mr Anderson and his first aid it could have been for good, the doctor said. All my eyelashes is gone. And my fringe! And what have the police done? Nothing!'

'Worse than nothing!' Mrs Taylor was determined to speak her mind. 'That sergeant - what was his name, Clara? The bloke with the big hooter? Ramsbotton! He had the cheek to accuse me of going for her with a red-hot salamander! Just because it was to hand on the table. Me! I showed 'im!'

'A red-hot what?' Redfyre asked, bemused.

She pointed to an instrument of torture, iron spikes running along an iron stem with a very long handle.

'Can't say I blame him, madam! Just the sight of it makes me want to confess. To anything.'

Ida laughed. 'Get it red hot and it's just what you need to crisp the top of a crème brûlée. But that iron had been cleaned and put on one side to cool hours before! Everybody knows that sweet has to sit and chill in the fridge after you've caramelized it. Hah! If that iron had been still hot, I'd have Ramsbottomed him all right!'

'Ouch! You were fortunate that the police were so quickly on the scene, I think?'

'Well you'd expect them to get a move on, considering who the master was entertaining!' Ida Taylor had commented. 'Didn't they tell you, love, who was here that night?'

'I think you have every right to complain, Miss Croft,' Redfyre had said before taking his leave. 'Look here - I think, from your account, I can guess the identities of the guilty parties. The police will have the cuffs on them by tomorrow and you won't ever be bothered again. Them!

Yes. There were two of them involved, I do believe. There's one more person to see before I can be quite certain. Tell me, Clara, does Alfred's employer keep a butler or a housekeeper?'

* * *

The superintendent turned to Redfyre with a smile. '*Two* blokes? You want us to arrest two?'

'Yes, sir.' Trying to keep a straight face, he said: 'Sorry I can't supply the actual name for the fellow who goes by the stage name of "Draco, the Dragon-Man of Draconia", but I'm sure if you send in the troops to the next watering-hole of Bellamy's Circus and Fun-Fair, they will be able to identify him and extract it. They've moved on to Surrey, I understand, following their annual stint at the May-Day Fair on the Common. Mister Draco, you will find, is an adept at walking - and vaulting! - on stilts. And his breath is to be avoided. It will stink of inflammable fuel and his aim is uncertain. Just be careful when you move in to feel his collar.'

The governor was reining in his amusement. 'Accounts for the leap over the gate and the singeing... what about the white face? And those glowing eyes?'

'Stage make-up, sir. White face, exaggerated red mouth. And a pair of protective goggles. The glass reflected the flames and it looked as though his eyes were burning. His trick is to fill his mouth with the fuel and breathe it out while igniting it with a Zippo lighter. Not in the same league as a flame-thrower but devastating if the victim is caught up in the blast. I saw the effects on poor little Clara Croft. And the mental damage must be considerable - it was a shocking sight to encounter after dark in your back yard.'

'But why? Why go to all this bother to frighten a few maids?'

'Vengeance, sir. The man behind this, a vindictive, unpleasant toe-rag called Alfred who will be found in the bar at the George, decided to use his spare cash on being revenged on the girls he thought had ganged up on him and lost him his job. According to the housekeeper who had the training of him - for her sins! - he was "forever gallivanting". He'd spent hours up on the Common when the funfair arrived to set up shop the week before and bragged of making friends there. This was the real reason for wanting to be rid of him. He was wayward and unreliable. The formal complaint from the neighbours was seized on as a more concrete and acceptable excuse.

'Alfred went to the fun-fair and saw something he really liked in Mister Draco's performance. He stayed out late drinking with his new mate and ended up hiring the Dragon-man to join him in giving the girls the fright of their lives. They waited carefully for a couple of days after the fair departed and then struck. Twice only. Against the two girls whom Alfred chiefly blamed for his downfall: Clara and Annie. The last two reports were fabricated. For drama... to enliven dull lives... to back up their friends' stories... Mostly, I fear because the girls felt lonely and exposed out there. It was an excuse for giving in your notice. A girl has to have a solid reason for quitting her post if she ever wants to be employed again.'

'But hadn't the girls seen the performance for themselves? Wouldn't they have recognised a fire-eater when they saw one?'

'The performances fell on weekdays, sir. These are live-in girls - skivvies - in day-long employment. Their day off, if they are so lucky as to have one, is a Sunday. None of them had been to the fair.'

'Congratulations, Redfyre!' The governor beamed at him. 'Puzzle solved, I think! In double quick time.'

'No, sir. The *crime* is solved. Spring-Heeled Jack was easy enough to unmask. Any one of the men on the case could have put two and two together, as I did, from talking to the girls involved, had they considered it worth their notice... had they seen it as the crime it was and not just as an outbreak of female hysteria. They simply did not bother to pay attention. They caught sight of a salamander on the kitchen table and assumed a bit of domestic fringe-singeing had gone on in house so to speak. No. The *puzzle* is: why on earth you sent me galloping about at Chief' Constable Benson's behest.'

'No need to pursue this, Redfyre.'

'Need? Perhaps not. But I'm interested. C.C. Benson and his lady wife, I discovered from Clara and Ida Taylor, were actually dining at the house in question on the night in question. The owner - who also happened to be the developer of the whole project - had sold plot number seven, I believe, to none other than Benson. Foundations already laid. Investment of a goodly sum of money made. Why don't you ring the Chief up and tell him that his chosen property is now safe from rumours of violence, mayhem and long-leggety beasties. Its value will be preserved. And his wife will be untroubled by an exodus of fearful maidservants.'

'Were you aware, Redfyre,' the superintendent was straining to hold back a guffaw, 'that you have this in common with our miscreant: when you open your mouth, you can deliver a scorcher? Well, I suppose you should always fight fire with Fyre. Or so they say.'

Cambridge Present

Kill Me Tomorrow

The watcher crouched behind rubbish bins overflowing with a fortnight's stinking detritus. The warm weather had come early to Cambridge this year and was causing him some discomfort. He stealthily changed his position, eased his limbs and averted his nose, trying to catch a fresh breeze down the alley-way.

At least he had something pleasant to distract and occupy his other senses.

He allowed his gaze to be drawn back to the two girls standing, arms around each other's waist, teetering on the edge of the pavement. Well why not? Everyone within a hundred yards of them was staring at the couple. Skimpy skirts and death-defying heels - the summer uniform of the Cambridge Working Girl. You couldn't get away any longer with calling them 'prostitutes'. The public felt more comfortable with the delusion created by the use of the innocent-sounding 'girls', and 'working' suggested reassuringly that they might even be paying income tax.

This pair were shouting cheerful insults and invitations at the drivers of cars braking for the bend where they'd positioned themselves. Unsuccessfully so far. Most had slowed dramatically to look at the girls; some had leaned over and shouted encouragement or lascivious promises. None had suggested serious business. The watcher shook his head in an expression of knowing irony. What else did they expect? On a Saturday afternoon, these blokes had other things on their mind. They were on their way to a football match. And not just any match - the next

Cup round was being played at the local ground up the road. Sex would always take second place to football. Breathing took second place to a Cup fixture.

To relieve his boredom, the watcher indulged in a little fantasy. Blonde or redhead if he had the choice? Any man's first impulse would be towards the blonde. Tall and slender with a cloud of shoulder-length fair hair, she reminded him of the angel on his grandma's Christmas tree - until she opened her mouth. He shuddered with distaste as the angel let rip with a stream of obscene invective in exchange for a White-Van-Man's provoking comments. Wherever had she learned such language? His granny would have known how to deal with *her*! A Coal-tar soap mouthwash and the cupboard under the stairs for the night! Vicious old trout, his Gran. He winced at the memory. But she'd have stood none of this nonsense. He almost looked furtively over his shoulder, fearing still the old lady's challenge. 'Gary! Is that *you* skulking by the bins? Come out at once and show me your hands!'

Gran wouldn't have thought much of the redhead either but she was Gary's choice. Not immediately as attractive but you'd probably have a more interesting time with this one. Shorter, more rounded, with all the cockiness of a back-yard robin. Shantelle, she called herself. That was her street name. Her friend was Christalle. He'd heard them calling to each other when one or the other went off round the corner for a coffee. Enjoying the game. Stupid, really. Who did they think they were kidding? With their unblemished complexions, smooth limbs and freshly-washed hair, no one but a fool would take them for real tarts. The pros on this beat had empty eyes, raddled faces and strawky hair and they covered up the needle tracks with long sleeves and jeans. Still - their male clients were pretty damn thick and self-deceiving... they were easily dazzled and incapable of thinking twice about the genuineness of what was on offer. They'd buy a lottery ticket, bet on a horse, pick up a blonde by the roadside and always believe it was nothing but their due. Their lucky day.

No surprise there but the question that niggled him was - why weren't these two chancers being seen off with the usual territorial aggression by the regular girls? Granted, there'd been many fewer working the streets in this part of Cambridge since the murders had started. Most had sought shelter in the safe houses opening up in the quiet residential streets off Eastern Avenue and the ones left pounding the pavements were grouping together in twos and threes for some sort of protection. When one was picked up and driven off, her friend would ostentatiously write down the number in a notebook. The clients objected and there'd been a fracas or two resulting in even less activity on the street.

The regulars were not in evidence today. Warned off? Or stunned by the latest murder - the fourth of what was beginning to look like a series. A corpse had been dragged out of a ditch to the south of the city, yesterday. Strangled, like the others.

They were beginning to call him the Clock Killer. Some clever dick brought in from the Metropolitan Police had plotted the dumping grounds or the 'deposition locations' as they called them these days, and come up with the theory that the man responsible was working his way around what would look like a clock face with Cambridge at the centre. The first girl had been killed and left in the Fens to the north at the number twelve on the dial. The second had been found in a country lane at ten past, the third south of Newmarket at twenty past and this latest due south on a golf course by the Gog-Magog hills. And all equidistant from the red light area where they'd been picked up. A ten mile radius.

The Brainiac from the Met had treated the media to a

learned explanation of the compulsion that led to a villain choosing his spots with such (literal) clockwork precision. The watcher gave a thin smile. He knew better. These days every Tom, Dick and Harry watched CSI programmes. Profiling, DNA analysis, trace evaluation... there were no more professional secrets. But the police went on assuming their man was an out-of-control noddy. The truth was - the perp was well clued-up about crime location diagrams, comfort zones, crime commission intervals and all the rest of the semi-scientific garbage. The watcher knew exactly what he was up to. By sticking to a pre-arranged pattern, the killer was side-stepping any attempt at analysis and concealing his base. He needn't be the local man they had projected. He could be any London man with a map. It was as simple as that.

The media had caught on to the clock face, of course. The headlines had screamed out the question: '*Who will be the 40 minute victim? Is time running out for number* 5?'

The *Cambridge Observer* had printed out a diagram plotting the crime spots radiating out from the red light zone and, in heavy type: the number 8. It hadn't taken much calculation to work out that west-south-west, ten miles distant and right under the number 8, lay the innocent, sleepy village of Foxfield. Sleepy no longer. The local inn was stuffed to the gunwales with press and police, tripping over each other in their fervid expectation of the next crime.

The watcher's smile widened. Not much chance of an abduction given the level of surveillance. A smart bloke, the killer would no doubt call it a day and turn his attention to another town. Peterborough, perhaps? Lively scene up there, he'd heard. Unless an unmissable opportunity presented itself here. He glanced again at the two girls by the roadside and calculated the risks. Just how vulnerable were they? He noted the CCTV camera above his head. Trained on the girls. A hundred other cameras covered every inch of this street. And, on the tree-lined road parallel to the main avenue there was a mobile police headquarters van parked on a patch of waste ground. Only a complete idiot would fall to the lure offered by these gaudy girls.

Decoy ducks. Police detectives, both. They weren't risking much. Trained in unarmed combat, the pair of them. The watcher was a big, strong lad but he'd have thought twice about tangling with them. And the girls were secure in the knowledge that every shrub, every dumpster, and every corner had a police constable lurking behind it doing nothing but watch them. Overkill. Waste of time.

Every man they could call on had been brought in for the operation. Even auxiliaries like himself - Community Police Officer Gary Newstead - had been taken off regular duties and put to work on the investigation. Still, he wasn't complaining. Watching Shantelle and Christalle larking about - it beat nicking shoplifters in the Arboretum Estate mini-mart. And the overtime was always welcome.

He'd thought they were on to something earlier. Thick traffic in both directions. Surely the top brass could have liaised with someone and found there were events going on all over the city this Saturday? A smart Bentley had cruised by, returning within minutes. A gent had stepped out, actually stepped *out* of the car to address the girls. His booming voice had carried as far as Gary even over the street noise, relaxed and conversational: 'I say, ladies! I find myself encumbered by a growing problem. Any chance of a some assistance, I wonder? From one of you? Both?' Gary's crouch had moved smoothly into a racing start. He'd noticed that the gent's eyes were sharp and were taking in his surroundings. Cute as an alley-rat, this one. He must have sensed that something was not quite right; the voice, when he spoke again, no longer had its confident edge. 'Lost my way, I fear. Sat-nav absolutely useless! I'm trying to get to the shindig at the hospital... dashed if I can remember its name...They've got a red-ribbon fund-raiser on. Know the one I mean...?'

Shantelle, popping her gum and grinning, had directed him to turn around and head back east and pick up the Newmarket road where he'd find the Cambridge Clinic. And that had been the only excitement.

Newstead pulled up the cuff of his special-issue police camouflage suit and checked his watch. Nearly two hours here and no result. Two more hours to go. He stifled a yawn.

His attention sharpened. Something happening at last?

He relaxed again. The redhead was whispering in the ear of her mate and giggling. He interpreted the body language. She was apologetically nipping off to the van for a quick pee.

'Don't do anything I wouldn't do while I'm away, Christalle!' she shouted with annoying archness.

Newstead cringed. His professional sensitivities were affronted. 'Stupid cows! They were enjoying themselves too much. Centre of attention and fancying themselves in the role. Well, all women were tarts at heart. He'd often heard it said. Why couldn't she cross her legs? Or lay off the coffee? She should have thought! This manoeuvre was unscheduled - could put the whole operation at risk. All this detailed planning and someone forgot that girls need to go to the loo, especially when they're feeling nervous.

He watched Shantelle hurry fifty yards down the road but his head whipped back to the pavement in front of him at the sound of screeching tyres. A black taxi had drawn up right by the other girl, Christalle. Gary Newstead tensed as the blonde put her head on one side, peered, and moved forward to greet the driver. He counted himself an expert on reading body language and he could have sworn he spotted the exact moment the girl realised she knew the driver. Gary stayed uncertainly in place. No one else was moving in. Was this some police manoeuvre that hadn't filtered down to bottom-feeders like him?

The driver of the black London cab leaned over, flung the door open and began to speak to the girl. She was showing surprise but no sign of tension or fear. She leaned in close and talked back to him. This must be prearranged. Plain-clothes inspector calling by to take her pizza order? Just what he'd expect of this Keystone Cops op! The watcher decided he could stand down.

Abruptly, he froze, hardly able to believe what he was seeing.

The driver was hauling the blonde into the passenger seat. All Gary got was a glimpse of a black-shirted arm, a black watch strap and a dark head. He heard the click of the doors as the automatic lock was applied. The cab drove off at speed.

No time to juggle with notebooks. Shaking off his astonishment, Gary pulled his pen from his pocket and scribbled down the number of the vehicle on his wrist, then he charged forward to join all the other ineffectual lurkers breaking cover, red in the face and stammering excuses for their lapse.

'Did anyone get the number?'

'Where's the bloody pursuit car?'

'Get on to traffic control!'

'Alert the team at Foxfield!'

'Ten miles away. He won't get that far but check the backstop's in place!'

In the hubbub, Special Constable Gary Newstead finally made his voice heard. 'I got it, sir! Sir! I got the number!'

* * *

'For your own safety, sir...' The blonde girl's voice had an edge of steel. 'I'd advise you to stop and put me out at once.'

'What?' The driver's response was derisive. 'Before I've sampled the wares on offer? You're very choosy for a tart, aren't you?' He cast a scathing look sideways. 'I'm assuming that's what you are? Decked out in that bum-freezing bit of titillation, with hair gilded and frizzed and starched to a standard any medieval Florentine light-skirt would have envied! Just don't insult me by telling me you were conducting a traffic survey or collecting for charity! Why the sudden shyness? Could it be that you don't perform for old acquaintances?'

Detective Constable Stella Kenton sighed and tried to assess the determination and aims of the stern-faced man at the wheel of the black cab. The latest in a line of extraordinary vehicles he'd owned. She remembered ten years ago it had been a Thunderbird, followed by an e-type Jaguar, then an ancient and totally covetable Morgan. Always more than a touch of the showman about Julius Jameson.

She tried again. 'It's not what you think. No time to explain, even if I were allowed to. Drop me here. Right here. At once. You've put yourself in danger.'

'Ah! You're threatening me with your poxy pimp? Ooh, I shake with terror!'

The wheel of the taxi wobbled dramatically and she bit back a nervous protest.

With creeping alarm, Stella had noticed that he was threading his way skilfully through the city, moving with the typical panache of a taxi, one of the hundreds on the road on a busy Saturday. No one looked twice at a cab shooting down a side-street or driving up a bus-lane. It was what cabs did. They were making excellent speed but going where? The green square of Parker's Piece came into view, edged on its eastern side by the grim grey slab of Police Headquarters. For a hysterical moment she thought he was about to dump her at the desk and turn her in. She'd never live it down. But the station passed by on the right and all lights changed in their favour as they approached. Over the river and on to the common, dotted with black and white cows up to their udders in a froth of Queen Anne's Lace.

There could be no doubt. He was heading south west, out into the country. She knew where he was taking her. But could he possibly have remembered - after ten years?

He broke her tense silence as they joined the Barton road. 'Do you think, you little twerp, that I knocked myself out for two years getting you and those other bumpkin friends of yours through their A levels and on to University for you to end up tarting on the street? Where did I go wrong? What's the attraction? Do tell!'

His cynical purr had always set her teeth on edge. The other girls had thought it sexy. They'd sighed when he'd recited Shakespeare to the class - and Mr Jameson never passed up a chance to use his voice. An actor turned teacher when the roles had dried up, he'd had the looks, the glamour and the confidence to reduce the class to a jelly. But Stella had never been taken in by the sculpted profile, the ready wit, the throbbing baritone. With Mr. Jameson, all was, she was convinced, illusion. She'd always pictured him as a mysterious box swathed in black velvet. But when you stripped the layers off, what was inside? Emptiness - or a picture of himself?

'Getting much job satisfaction, are you?' He'd not lost the knack of irritating her to the point of fury.

'Plenty,' she couldn't restrain herself from saying lightly. She decided he didn't deserve an explanation. And he'd only laugh even more derisively if she told him she was a detective constable. He'd always affected a disdain for the conventional, the conservative, the mundane. He'd projected a bohemian image, perpetually surprised and disconcerted to find himself in a classroom. No, she'd stay in the character she'd assumed, the better to torment him. 'The financial reward is much better than anything you could get from teaching. And, honestly, there's not a lot you can do with a degree in English, is there, sir?' She regretted that the automatic 'sir' had slipped out.

'Honestly?' he spoke with emphasis. 'No, I suppose not. You chose the *dis*honest and lazy option, I see. Don't you want to know where I'm taking you?'

She didn't answer but she was quite certain she knew. She would have to brace herself for an uncomfortable scene when they got there. He wasn't taking her back to her city flat. He had no way of knowing where she lived. He was heading out to the country to one of the villages ten miles away to the south-west. To her mother's house at Shepton. He was going to dump her on her mother's doorstep again just as he had ten years ago. And deliver another telling off.

Then, it had been a gently finger-wagging: 'Afraid your daughter's had a little too much to drink at the disco, Mrs Kenton. I'm sure you'll find the right words to say to her... when she's sober enough to hear them, of course. We wouldn't want this to happen again, would we?'

And *this* time what would he come up with? 'Found your daughter selling sexual services on the streets, Mrs Kenton. I'm sure you'll find the words to discourage further excursions into immorality.'

Stella suppressed a giggle. Her mother was smart. She'd take the situation in at once, feel embarrassed for his mistake, make all the right conversational noises, and the upshot would be the same as last time. When he'd refused her polite offer of a cup of tea and left, she and her Mum would stand in the hall, eyeing each other until they heard the sound of his car moving off and they'd fall about laughing.

He enjoyed her silence and then said: 'I think you've guessed.'

He put his foot on the accelerator, sliding neatly between lorries heading for the motorway. Then, at the last moment, he nipped down a side-street, turned and re-entered the traffic flow in the opposite direction. 'Turn on a sixpence, these cabs,' he announced cheerfully. 'I shall never drive anything else. You can get them for a song, you know, at the London car auctions. Change of seating arrangements essential, of course.' He cast a satisfied glance at the passenger seat with its leather upholstery. 'Rather unfriendly to carry people about in the back. A quick change of license plates and you're anonymous. Never get stopped by the Plod.' He cleared his throat. 'Change of plan,' he added. 'I've decided what to do with you.'

'Whatever it is, this is kidnap. You are holding me here against my will and I have given you due warning.' She was proud of the firmness of her tone.

Her abductor was less impressed, apparently. 'Who's going to listen to the bleatings of a common prostitute? Come off it! Occupational necessity, isn't it - getting into cars with men? But this is your lucky day. I came along quite by chance and I may even be able to save you from a lifetime of sin. Who knows? Life's too short and too precious to spend it in the gutter.' He flashed another cold glance. 'On drugs are you? No? Surprised but pleased to hear that. You're not too far gone. You look as though there might still be time to save you from yourself, as they say.'

He gave a short bark of laughter. 'Remember Henry IV?

the time of life is short;
To spend that shortness basely were too long,
If life did ride upon a dial's point,
Still ending at the arrival of an hour.
An if we live, we live to tread on kings;
If die, brave death, when princes die with us!

'Dial? Hour? Death?' The words tolled like a funeral knell in her head and Stella felt a trickle of cold horror creep along her spine.

For the first time since he'd picked her up, it occurred to her to wonder what business he could possibly have, driving down Eastern Avenue through the red light district. Sick in her heart, she realised that this man whom she had always mistrusted, was not taking her home to her mother in Shepton as she had naively assumed. He seemed to have other plans for her.

* * *

The Detective Inspector was trying to keep the lid on the pot of bubbling emotions. 'That's enough, Shantelle! Er... Katy! Not your fault. When Nature calls and all that... Not one hundred per cent your fault... let's say forty-nine. Fifty one for Stella. Why the hell didn't she put up a fight or get off a scream? She's always ready enough to have a go at me... Something not right here... Get me the replays up on screen. We'll take another gander. Where's that cab got to? You're joking! Hell! He's given us the slip? Anyone traced the number? A *London*-registered cab?' He groaned. 'A poacher! That's all we need! Now we'll have the Met swarming all over our patch! Track 'im! He's most likely on the M11 by now, heading south.'

An exclamation of dismay from the redhead distracted him.

'Oh, for God's sake, Katy! Look, love, do us all a favour, will you, and stop blubbing! Go home. Take the rest of the shift off. After you've made your statement. Go back to the station... you're in no fit state... is there a squad car around? Get someone to give you a lift back, love...' He paused and added awkwardly, seeing her shoulders shake: 'Try not to worry! She'll be all right. Tough girl,

77

D.C. Kenton. Go and put some clothes on - that'll make you feel better.'

The Inspector waved her away. The sympathetic eyes of the rest of the squad followed her as, white-faced and suddenly awkward, Katy slipped a pink cardigan over her bare shoulders and stumbled out of the office in her sparkling high heels.

* * *

He veered unexpectedly off the west-bound road again.

'*Now*, where are you going? I'm getting fed up with this!'

'You know where. But first, we're going to drive around for a bit. Get to know each other again. I want to hear your story, Stella. Find out what led you into this disgusting mess. Try to understand. You may not have guessed it, but you were always one of my favourite students. Not the cleverest - but the most individual.'

'You disguised your esteem pretty well,' she said, unbelieving.

'I'm good at disguise,' he reminded her.

They drove out into the country, past the fruit farms. They passed a signpost to the left: *Shepton 6 miles Foxfield 6 miles.*

'Your neck of the woods, if I remember rightly?' he commented.

He drove straight on. 'I thought we'd go via Grantchester.' Suddenly he was speaking with the heavy kindliness of an uncle proposing an outing. 'Such a beautiful village. All of England is there, I always think. Now, if one were dying, these are the images one would want to carry with one, wouldn't you agree?'

'One would agree,' she replied, determined to be tiresome.

'I'd want to say goodbye with, imprinted on my mind's eye, meadows full of moon-pennies, chestnut trees,

78

swans preening on mysterious dark stretches of river, a dappled horse bolting away into the woods and... and... here it comes now! The church! Check the time, Stella - I don't want to take my eyes off the road... tricky bend coming up... wouldn't be much fun if we both ended up splattered on the churchyard wall, would it? But it wouldn't be bad to be hearing the words of Rupert Brooke as one expired, either...What was it he said?

Stands the church clock at ten to three?
And is there honey still for tea?
Well, go on! Have a look!'

'Of course it stands at ten to three!' she snarled, annoyed by his dramatics. 'Because it *is* ten to three! You stage-managed that well.' She dared to ask: 'Do you ever stop acting and just... well... *live*?'

The question provoked a laugh he would probably himself have described as 'sepulchral', she thought. It boomed out from some cold, empty space.

'And why this obsession with time?'

'I think I've already answered your question. Or, at least, The Bard has spoken for me. That's why he's so often quoted, Stella. Whatever our deepest thoughts, you can be sure that Shakespeare has already voiced them for us but with ten times the nobility of phrase. If only we had the wit to profit by his wisdom, how many mistakes we would avoid, how much pain would be averted. Your own life, for instance – would you say it "rode upon a dial's point"?'

Stella groaned. Why, after all these years, did she feel he was still testing her? With a strange feeling that her response might be important for her also, she wrestled with memory and expression.

'Okay, here comes your answer: the speaker in your passage is the King, I guess, because he's using the royal "we". He's saying life's short. So we ought to live as good a one as we're able. If we live on, well, that gives us an advantage over any dead king because you can take nothing with you when you go - not even kingly status. And if we die - so what? - it's a brave death when princes are dying along with us.'

Jameson gave an elegant shudder. 'Something on those lines,' he said repressively.

She looked again at the face, as handsome as it had been ten years ago, but subtly changed. The cheeks were hollowed, the long-lashed dark eyes were shadowed, the mouth indecisive, tormented. Well, it was pretty much as you'd look if you'd decided to kill someone, she supposed.

But her training was taking over. She flexed her hands and feet ready to call on instant supplies of adrenaline when the moment came for flight or fight. If she could only get out of the car and kick off her silly shoes, she thought she could probably outrun him. And, though he was strongly built, she'd put up a fight if it came to it. This victim wouldn't go down without a murmur. There'd be tissue under finger nails, scratches on his face. She decided on a surprise pre-emptive attack, going for the eyes. While his hands were still on the wheel. He'd never expect it. But there was something she could try first. She was a sort of hostage, wasn't she? Okay - she'd try out the prescribed technique. She might just pull it off. Avoid bloodshed. After all, it was unknown for serial killers to murder someone they already knew. She'd have to work that for all it was worth. Stop baiting him. Establish a rapport. Stella buttoned her blouse, pulled down her skirt, settled back in her seat and looked out of the window.

'You're right, Mr Jameson - I say, may I call you Julius? after all these years I feel I've caught up with you in age - it *is* perfection. Glorious countryside! And the best moment of the year! Easy to see why neither of us has moved away.'

(A small link but worth mentioning.)

'And I may not be looking the part at the moment but I have actually stayed a scholar of sorts. I played Desdemona in my first year in College...You inspired me - you inspired many of us... did you know Maisie Smith was madly in love with you, by the way? No? And Jennifer Hogg and Patrick Dewar? We were sure you must have guessed!

(Feed his sense of self-importance.)

'Now this time when you deliver me to Mum, I want you to accept her cup of tea. Lots to talk about!'

(Convey the idea that the man has a future beyond the present circumstances.)

Stella added an incentive her instructors had never thought of: 'Yesterday was baking-day... there'll be a Victoria sponge and some chocolate brownies.'

(Greed. What man could ever resist a brownie?)

Her girlish prattle faded away. His eyes were looking inward, dull and dark as Byron's Pool, and she realised he hadn't taken in a word she'd said. He turned to her. The swift smile he gave her was the sweetest she would ever encounter and was the more striking for its utter sincerity. Finally, he had dropped the mask of irony and she was being given a glimpse of the man below. But the face had frozen over again in agony, the man adrift and unapproachable.

'I'm glad you're with me at the last, Stella,' he said softly. 'I'd never have planned for it but now the moment's come, it feels right. I did always admire you, you know. Enjoyed our fencing bouts. If things had been different... Ah, well... *brave death when princes die with us.* A princess would have been good. But I'll settle for a tart. Whatever... it's nice to have company.'

She knew the signpost well. A few yards before the level crossing they were offered: *Shepton 1 mile Foxfield 1 mile.* He took the Foxfield turn, brought the taxi to a halt in the deserted lane facing the level crossing, looked at his watch and listened.

The three thirty train on the London line screeched its customary warning.

* * *

Gary Newstead scooped up the Monday copy of the *Cambridge Observer* from the mat and settled down with his mug of tea at the scrubbed table of his Gran's old kitchen. He grunted at the size of the headlines on the front page. Plenty of news today, then.

Fifth slaying! They shrieked.

Body found at Eight Bells Public House.

In a quiet village ten miles south-west of Cambridge, a day after she was reported missing, the latest victim of the Clock Killer has been found.

Almost exactly where experts predicted.

A police spokesman tells the 'Observer' that the corpse of a young woman had been abandoned, (possibly killed) in the orchard to the rear of the Eight Bells pub in Shepton. The modus operandi conforms to that of the four previous victims. There was no sign of sexual assault and the death was by strangulation.

Police fear that the killer, by the significance of his choice of location (EIGHT Bells), may be taunting the forces of law and order.

It had been widely predicted that the next attack would take place at nearby Foxfield which lies exactly on the number eight spot of the dial the police themselves had foreseen. It was late on Saturday night when the landlord became suspicious that something was amiss.

The pub's guard-dog, released to perform his nightly duties, entered the rear snug, carrying a lady's silver shoe in his mouth.

The Alsatian (Butch) led his master and a selection of guests outside to the next grisly find by torchlight: a pink cardigan caught up on a rose bush.

Behind the bush, the grim discovery.

A double shock awaited the investigating officers who hurried to the scene. An examination of the body revealed the victim to be one of their own. DC Katy Sharpe (25) who had, by a strange quirk of fate, herself been working on the case.

DCI Rowe who has been leading the enquiry will pay his respects to the deceased in a news conference to be held at noon today.

It is confidently expected that he will be announcing the arrest of a suspect.

The landlord, who is helping the police with their enquiries, told our reporter of his puzzlement. His pub, isolated and at the end of a cul-de-sac, had seen no traffic other than regulars and police vehicles coming and going at the weekend...

Gary read the article again carefully. He was so absorbed he didn't hear their quiet arrival.

'Enough shock-horror in there to entertain you, Newstead?' The grating voice of the Detective Inspector. 'Did they get it right?' Two heavy hands descended on his shoulders. He listened in silence to the rigmarole: 'Gary John Newstead, we are arresting you for the murder of Katy Sharpe....'

'Gerraway with you! You're 'aving a larf!' Newstead started to protest.

They couldn't know! He'd offered her a lift back to the station and no one had even noticed them set off. So many squad cars milling about they hadn't been given a second glance. They'd never trace the car. He couldn't even remember which one he'd used himself. She'd come quiet as a lamb, believing every word of the story he'd fed her about instructions to redeploy to Foxfield. Her mind was still on her mate. She was even keen to get there and help out. He'd knocked her unconscious in a lay-by before they approached the village and fastened her arms behind her back. His usual m.o. He risked no scrapings from finger-nails, no scratches on his face. Nasty moment when she'd come round in the shrubbery but he was always a quick, neat worker. He'd left no more trace than with any of the other sluts. And she *was* a slut. No doubt about that. He'd watched her enjoying herself, tormenting the men. Making fools of them. A slut.

Like his mother.

Gran had had to throw her out in the end. Then Gran had got him out of the Home and brought him up herself. Strictly. Correctly. She'd have approved.

The DI was trying to balance distress at the death of a smart young officer and elation at the result he was about to announce. His voice was tightly controlled and betrayed only a trace of glee as he allowed himself the satisfaction of an explanation.

'Katy was tough and she was clever. She worked out she was in trouble and left a trace in the police car. We checked out the whole bloody fleet! The one you were seen returning to the pool - the one that still has your finger-prints on the wheel also had - stuck down on the door side of the passenger's seat - a wodge of chewing gum. Cram full of Katy's DNA! She parked it there deliberately, I reckon.'

'Only proves I gave her a lift back to the station,' Newstead objected. 'Am I saying I didn't? If you ask me, I'll tell you! Go on - ask!'

'Agreed. But it was the first link. And once we had you up on screen, so to speak, it turns out it's the second link that's going to do for you... Tissue under her nails.'

The DI watched Newstead's face closely as he said the words.

Seeing with gratification the surprise he'd caused: 'Naw, lad! Not her *finger*nails. Tied behind her back with plastic cuffs, her hands were, to prevent any such give-away, but our Katy fought back as best she could, didn't she, Gary, old chap? In the only way left to her. She kicked off her shoes and raked your leg with her *toe*nails. I bet if I could work up the will to do it, I could lift your trouser leg and find a six inch scar on your ankle. Probably thought it was a rose bush you'd scratched yourself on in the scuffle? We've done the analysis. Now we'll be needing a sample of your DNA. Open wide, will you? Sergeant - if you please?

* * *

Mrs Kenton put the kettle on and hurried to answer the doorbell.

Her neighbour, round-eyed, thrust a copy of the local paper at her. 'Here you are, Sue. Page 3. What a tragedy! Ever so sorry, dear. Better not keep you, in the circumstances.' And she hurried off.

Sue Kenton settled down at the kitchen table with a pot of tea to read the account.

Angel of Death Flies over Village.

Second mysterious death in twenty four hours.

Has the Angel of Death flown over Shepton this weekend?

This is the question villagers are asking themselves as they grieve for a second local person whose dramatic death is reported.

A young Detective Constable whose family lives in the village, Stella Kenton (26), witnessed the tragic event.

Walking in a quiet country lane near her home, she was surprised, on approaching the Foxfield level crossing,

to be overtaken by a black taxi cab.

'The driver must have seen the lights flashing and the bar come down,' states the witness. 'Everything mechanical appeared to be working perfectly. The driver hesitated and waited until the goods train drew near and then he charged forward deliberately into its path.'

The taxi was swept a quarter of a mile down the track. It's a miracle that no one but the cab-driver was killed.

The driver of the train was taken to hospital suffering from shock but later released.

The victim was 38 years old actor Julius Jameson who will be remembered for his appearances as a young surgeon in the popular East Anglian series, 'Cottage Hospital'. Co-incidentally, Mr Jameson was, in recent years, actively concerned in real life in hospital affairs. He was one of the moving forces in the red-ribbon AIDS charity

Minutes later, Stella appeared, still in her dressing gown, pale and distressed. She'd shown every sign of bearing up well after the death of her old schoolteacher but the news on Sunday of Katy's death had sent her into a shuddering and prolonged silence. She came and sat down by her mother's side to read.

'Mr Jameson wouldn't be pleased. Second billing. His death only makes it onto page 3 this morning,' said Mrs Kenton with asperity. 'You lied to them, Stella. You told *me* you were in the car with this nutter seconds before. Have you told me everything?'

'I told them the simplest thing. What I thought they'd believe. It's taken me a while to work it out for myself,' Stella said. 'He was going to kill us both.' Her voice was subdued, emotionless. 'I couldn't get through to him, Mum. He wasn't even listening. He'd decided I was some worthless whore who'd be better off dead. He was doing me a favour. And using me to ward off the loneliness. He could never function without an audience and I was unlucky enough to drop into the front seat of the stalls to witness his grande finale. His death scene.'

Her mother hugged her and poured out two mugs of tea. 'What made him change his mind and let you out?'

'I used the only words that would penetrate his delusions.' She smiled. 'Not *my* words. He would never have listened to any words of mine. It was The Bard, as he called him, who came riding to my assistance.'

In a pure, awed voice she repeated the lines:
'That death's unnatural that kills for loving.
Alas, why gnaw you so your nether lip?
Some bloody passion shakes your very frame:
These are portents; but yet I hope, I hope,
They do not point on me.'

'Good Lord! You were taking a risk, weren't you?' Mrs Kenton froze in alarm. 'That's Desdemona pleading for her life minutes before Othello kills her! And you're saying he heard you? Did he understand? What did he say?'

'He understood, all right! He was never one to miss a cue! He gave me Othello's response: *"Down strumpet!"*'

'Gawd!' her mother breathed, clutching her hand.

'And all I had in reserve was the very next line: *'Kill me tomorrow; let me live tonight!'*

'It didn't work for Desdemona, poor chick.'

'The train hooted its half mile signal. He burst out laughing, unlocked the doors and pushed me out into the lane. He gave one of those Shakespearean bows, you know, all fluttering hands, gleaming teeth and tossing curls, and barged through the crossing bars. End. Finis.'

'But why the hell...? I don't understand! At least I can see why he'd want to do away with himself... He'd had a virtual death sentence from the hospital and had chosen a quick end over a slow one. But why put *you* and a train-load of innocent people through all that? Why are suicides such selfish show-offs?'

'Well, *this* is why, Mum! Here I am, here we are, talking about his final flourish.' Stella spread her hands in a wide gesture. 'If he'd had a lonely death, unobserved by anyone, they might have thought he'd made a silly mistake, lost concentration, been blinded by the sun... Idiots drive through level crossings every month, don't they? Who would ever know that Julius Jameson had died with panache, handsome as the devil, laughing right in the face of Death?'

Stella's calm finally broke, her voice stricken and angry: 'He's left dozens of people bruised and shocked and he's left me for ever with that image of his last living moment branded onto my mind. He made sure that there was someone here below who'll never forget his farewell performance.'

But her mother was having none of it.

'Bollocks!' she said. And, surprisingly:

"All the world's a stage
And all the men and women merely players,
They have their exits and their entrances."

'Fine, Stella love. As far as you're concerned, the bugger's made his exit! Got that? He's off stage... through a trap door... up in smoke... whatever you can picture. Give the selfish prick one last slow hand-clap and bring the curtain down on him. And now what you've got to do is look forward to an *entrance*. Surely it's time for your Prince Charming to stroll on stage?'

No Picnic for Teddy Bears

'Do we *have* to? Mum! I'm *twenty* six years old - not six!'

Detective Constable Stella Kenton, surprised to catch herself in the middle of a childish whine, cut it short at once. But she began to drag her heels as they walked along Shepton High Street and looked up resentfully at the church tower where an exuberance of laughter and honking bicycle horns seemed to be breaking out. 'Oh, look at that! Their awful shindig seems to be under way already. We could cross over and pretend we haven't noticed?'

'Oh, go on, Stella! You're in plain clothes... jeans and t-shirt... yes, very plain - you won't frighten the little ones. And anyway, the whole village knows who you are and what you do. Front page of the Cambridge Evening News last month - you're the nearest thing we've got to a celebrity. The vicar might ask you to judge an event... see fair play... something of that sort.' Mrs Kenton seized her daughter's arm, clamped it and smiled guiltily before adding: 'And I did tell the Rev you'd be coming along. I've been sewing those wretched parachutes for the last month at the Busy Fingers pre-school sessions! I'd like *someone* to appreciate what I've done even if it's only a sniffy, supercilious daughter.'

Stella grinned and gave in. 'Parachutes? What are you on about? I thought you were threatening me with a Teddy Bear show?'

Mrs Kenton pointed to the church notice board as they drew alongside.

'*Teddy Bears' Parachute Drop,*' Stella read out. '*All entrants must have owners under the age of ten. Launch 12 noon.*' She glanced at the church clock. Half an hour to go. And there are the owners and trainers...' She laughed indulgently at the seething mob of children scrambling for places on the front row facing the drop target: a super-sized sheet with a bull's eye painted in the centre and pegged down onto the grass.

'Windy day!' her mother commented with satisfaction. 'That'll add to the excitement! Be lucky to land any of them on target.'

'And there they are, lining up on the parapet, loosely in the control of the vicar: the intrepid airmen.' Stella squinted into the sunshine, making out a black-gowned figure flitting about and doing a lot of arm-waving. 'That *is* the Rev Blandish up there?'

'That's him. He's so good with the children. They really love this event.'

'Poor old soul! The things he'll put himself through for the church fund! Oh, do be careful, Rev!' she muttered. 'One blast of wind up your cassock and you'll launch off with the bears! He just picks up the furry paras and chucks them off the tower does he? Ouch! That's no picnic for a teddy bear. I'm not sure I'd have let him do that to my Bruno when I was a kid.'

'Well some of them do experience a stab of regret when their little friend leaps into space and we can expect tears before touch-down. And... by the way, Stella... you might like to cast a professional eye... ever so discreetly... on the Low Road gang sitting on the wall over there.'

'So that's why I'm here! I'm a detective, Mum! Academy-trained élite crime-buster! I leave ASBO patrol to the beat force. And, besides, it's my day off.' Stella was laughing but her eyes were automatically running along the line of teenagers. 'Some ugly faces there, under the baseball caps! What are they doing here? They should be off

91

popping their lager cans behind the bus stop. You're not telling me that lot have any interest in flying bears?'

'Oh but they do! If you look closely you'll see them passing bits of paper about. They're running a book. They've learned how to do it from the gambling channels on the telly. They'll take your pound off you if you want to have a punt? Avoid Gary Sweet's *Paddington*... He's the favourite on account of his weighted wellies. He'll win but he'll be disqualified. Someone's already lodged a complaint with the vicar...' Stella's Mum smiled innocently. '*I've* got a quid on Emma's *Icarus*. He was runner-up last year and I know she's streamlined him since then. Sewed his legs together. More aerodynamic, you know. Clever little fingers with a needle... she caught on really fast...'

Stella sighed. 'Thanks for the tip. Remind me, Mum... is this the Church of All Saints or All Sinners?'

They entered the churchyard under a banner reminding all comers that the church needed desperately to raise a hundred thousand pounds for repairs to the roof. '*Another* hundred thousand? Didn't we just finish raising some huge sum last year?' Stella asked.

Stella's mum put on her stony face. 'This is in addition. To replace the roof lead and other metals pinched in the Spring. Toe-rags even took the lightning conductor! *And* the catalytic converter from under the Rev's Range Rover. It's a disgrace! Now, *that's* what your élite bunch *ought* to be doing - leaving the comfort zone of your computer keyboards and getting out onto the roof tops! Catching the villains! They're costing the county millions and does anyone ever round them up? Never! Everybody knows who's behind it - the Mister Big who runs the whole show from the safety of his smelting works over by the M11. And I bet your lot know who he is!'

Always wary of passing on information to her mother and unwilling to hear another boring 'Where's Sherlock

Holmes when you need him?' rant, Stella threaded her way through the tombstones towards the half dozen teenagers sitting with unnatural composure along the wall. Amongst the acned faces half hidden under baseball caps, she picked out the leader, greeted him pleasantly by name and asked to see a list of the runners. An eye-to-eye duel ensued, accompanied by shrugs, leers and protests of incomprehension. Stella stared him down and made a slight movement towards the shoulder bag where she kept her warrant card. 'All in a good cause, I'm told, Liam. Percentage of profits to the church roof fund, were you going to tell me? I'm cool with that. What do you say we keep a happy atmosphere for the kids? Your little bro got an entry, has he? Wouldn't want to find he'd been disqualified at the last minute.'

A grubby folded sheet of bears' names alongside a cross-hatching of altered betting odds was handed over. She spent a moment assessing it and made her choice. 'Put me down for a quid on *Biggles*.'

'Ooooh! Got a real punter 'ere lads!' An expression of scorn blended with surprise flitted across Liam's pale features. '*Biggles* eh?' He sucked his teeth to emphasise the trickiness of his calculation and then came to a magnanimous decision: 'We can give you ten to one on 'im... 'e's not much fancied.'

'Just the kind I like. No point backing the favourite is there?'

She left them hurriedly reassessing the odds on the dark horse *Biggles* and strolled off towards the church. Seeing her mother was already waist deep in a froth of excited children, Stella signalled that she was going to spend a few minutes in the church and she headed off to take shelter in the quiet gloom of the Norman nave.

She paused for a moment in the shelter of the porch to take out her mobile phone and dialled a Cambridge number. Speaking quietly, she identified herself and added: 'Just arrived on site. No problems so far.'

* * *

Passing into the church, she strolled by the font trailing a finger over the twelfth century carved limestone basin in which she'd been christened, enjoying the connection with the generations of villagers who'd shared the experience. A heritage worth handing on. She wondered if Liam and his gang placed any value on it. Her mother was right to be angry that, piece by piece, this precious connection was being stolen away. She would have been even more outraged if Stella had told her that her information on Mister Big was out of date. Lead and copper were finished. Government smelting licences and constant checks had cut the profits too low to be attractive. And Eddie Barnsdale's response had been to diversify.

It was thought he was getting into thefts of church artefacts. They hadn't all been knocked off in the eighties. There were plenty still remaining in the possession of remote country churches. A Saxon font would fetch a good price. Stella's eye ran an inventory over the carved oak candle-sticks flanking the altar, the brass vases, an impressive candelabrum. Huge and heavy but portable. And very covetable.

And most of these things never attempted a passage through Sotheby's. They were ticked off on some villain's shopping list and then redirected. Steal-to-order antiques. The silver plate was no longer stored in the village treasure chest; it had been sent off years ago to the museum in Cambridge for safe-keeping and display. The church was now kept locked but the parish notice board cheerfully announced that a key was available from any one of four keyholders who lived close by. Easy work for a 'visitor' to sign one out under a false name and knock off a copy. They'd return after dark with a lorry and four brawny blokes and nick all the objects their spotter had identified and marked on a plan. They'd be off down the motorway to London before you could say 'nave'.

Stella reviewed her briefing on the villain Barnsdale. Working anonymously through a series of cutouts, he'd recently made the mistake of taking a personal interest in antiquities. The missis was very keen on that sort of thing, it was rumoured. He'd taken to visiting the sites of interest with his wife as bona fide tourists, helping themselves to a plan of the church layout from a pile conveniently available on a table and pencilling in the precise position of the goodies they'd spotted. His strong-arm task executives wouldn't know a rood-screen from a radish but Annyetta, the third Mrs Barnsdale, knew all right.

A statuesque red-head with a degree in Marketing and Communications from Anglian College, she'd come to Barnsdale's attention as his Personal Assistant. She'd personally assisted him to get rid of his second wife and now graced his extravagant country house in uxorial rôle. And Annyetta never missed an episode of *Antiques Roadshow* they said.

The Barnsdale drawing room - or 'solar' as the chatelaine preferred to call it - had even made an injudicious appearance in a glossy magazine. Annyetta was to be discovered on page 62 of *An English Heaven*, the May edition, arranging lilies in a silver urn atop a Jacobean table of some distinction, in front of a painting of 'The Lady of Shallott' which, if it wasn't by some pre-Raphaelite painter, was a damned good imitation. The article had been brought to the attention of Stella's superintendent and the squad had been alerted.

In fact it was the lady's questionable desires that had further alerted the curate right here in All Saints, Shepton. Just last week this young man: handsome, sighed-after, single but unattainable James Lovelace, had come upon the two in the middle of their reconnaissance. In five minutes of 'Welcome to the church... are you local?' prattle the curate had heard warning bells ringing in his head. The lady of the pair was doing all the talking. Showing off. Flirting with him even.

'They will *do* that,' James had grumbled into the receptive ear of Superintendent Crackstone of the Cambridge CID. Keeping a polite reserve, the curate had, with a few clever questions, deduced that they were up to no good and that they knew far more about the portable elements of the church décor than a pair of innocent passing tourists ought to. They showed not the slightest interest in anything that was fixed and unmoveable. 'Hmm. Now what do you make of *that,* detective?' he'd wanted to know.

The information had eventually filtered down to the bottom of the pond where Stella lurked. Stirred to the surface by a phone call from DS Crackstone, her boss, early this morning: 'You live in Shepton, don't you Constable? Going anywhere near the church this morning are you? Wonder if you'd mind... as you're on the spot... Probably nothing to it but... Must be seen to respond... Have a word with the... what is he?... Ah, yes, curate... Some sort of rookie priest, would that be? Check him out. See if he's a reliable witness...'

Why did her colleagues assume that clergymen were unworldly, off-with-the-angels types? Stella grated out an icily polite response. 'Sir, James Lovelace is a graduate in astro-physics and mathematics. He divides his spare time between climbing Mount Everest, translating medieval Persian love poetry and singing in a rap band.' She flattered the young man with her outrageous invention but his credentials, she remembered from her mother's account, were certainly impressive and did indeed include mountain climbing. As well as his other attributes, the curate was awesomely athletic. It was said

- and always with an indulgent smile - that he'd commandeered the vestry and turned this useful space into a repository for his sporting gear which ranged from skis to hockey sticks. 'If James says he's identified a threat to the church contents or fabric - you'd better believe him. Sir.'

She realised she'd talked herself into giving up a free morning when the Super, after the slightest pause, had said comfortably: 'Oh? A fan are you? I shan't feel guilty, then, about asking you to go along and have a snoop around...'

And here she was, snooping.

And seeing nothing but quiet normality. She smiled dreamily up at the dust motes drifting in the sun's rays slanting through the clerestory, sniffed the familiar scent of white flowers and candles lightly underpinned by incense. The rising excitement from the churchyard was dulled to a dim background rumble by the thick fieldstone walls and for a moment Stella assumed she was alone in the body of the church.

A discreet cough and a sigh from the front of the nave told her otherwise and, with country good manners, Stella made her way down to greet the figure hunched over a low table in front of the parish chest in what everyone called 'the children's corner'.

'Janice! They've left you with the tidying - as usual? You're too good to them! Go on outside and watch the descent. They're just about to start.'

'Oh, that's no bother, Stella. And I've seen it all before. *Someone* has to sort this lot out and clean the finger-paint trays. It's been sitting about here since yesterday.' She sighed. '*James* is giving the sermon tomorrow. I wouldn't want him to look down from the pulpit and see all this mess.' She blushed and bent her head over the paint-trays, attacking the crusted layers with vigour.

Stella smiled. Janice Denbigh was one of nature's

Marthas. A really useful engine. A volunteer. Somewhere approaching dusty middle-age, she was a stalwart of the Busy Fingers under fives group. Always available, always exploited but always acknowledged. And it was this acknowledgement, Stella supposed, that motivated her to spend endless hours in the company of restless, noisy children. She'd been one of those children herself twenty years ago.

'Go on with you! I've got some time spare,' Stella heard herself saying. 'I'll put this lot away. You do too much, Janice.'

Janice glowed with satisfaction. 'If you'll help me with the lid, we can stack it all away in the play chest, Stella.' Stella smiled at the words as they sorted and piled. Play chest? A casual way of referring to the fifteenth century parish chest. There it lay, forming one of the boundaries of the play area. Eight feet long and carved in ancient oak, its majesty belied its current name and purpose. The front sported four deeply carved panels representing the elements of earth, air, fire and water. The four original locks were long gone and the lid, which could only be lifted by an adult, was fastened safely open during play sessions.

Preparing to raise the lid, Stella exclaimed: 'Oh Janice! Would you look at this? Some careless little twit's shoved his paint pot in there still full! Look it's leaked out!'

Janice exclaimed, came over and dropped to her knees to examine the spreading brown stain on the oak floor boards. 'Drat! Oh! It's all over the floor! And it's dried on! That'll be little Freddy! So absent-minded! He was mixing up a pot of mud colour for his farm-yard. He's always the first to finish. Can never wait around for the others. I bet he put his tray away without washing it. And in the wrong place! It's oozing out through the dust hole... you know the hole we had drilled in the bottom so we can brush all the dust to a corner and clean it out more easily. Let's hope he didn't slam it down on top of the dressing-up clothes!'

The two women eased the lid back to rest against the wall. They stood in silence for a moment. Finally, Stella, for the first time in her life, uttered an oath in church. Janice gurgled and gasped and began to buckle at the knees.

They stared down into the chest in horror.

Against a froth of pink tulle and blue satin, silver shoes and golden crowns, the body of a man stood out starkly in his formal dark suit. He was laid out on his back, arms crossed over his chest as if in a coffin. The head was hidden from view by a pair of crossed angels' wings, placed protectively over it. Ominously, the white feathers were stained here and there by the same red-brown fluid.

To peek or not to peek? There was no resisting the urge to lift the wings. With icy control, Stella rehearsed her speech to the Governor: '... any chance that the man was still alive... first aid might have been the necessary next step... Aloud, she said: 'Janice, this may be unpleasant. I advise you to look away. Why don't you go and sit down again?' But Janice gave her a blank stare and went on breathing heavily down her neck.

The face and head were almost unrecognisable. The victim had been savagely beaten and the now-dried blood flow had streamed copiously from the wounds to pond above Janice's drainage hole. Stella followed the trail of it with a pointing finger. 'Not mud but blood,' she murmured superfluously.

'Is he dead?' Janice whispered.

Jolted into a professional reaction by the unnecessary question, Stella put out a hand to touch a clean spot on the man's neck, trying to hide her distaste and affected to find a pulse point on the cold flesh. 'Dead. Some time ago.' She delicately replaced the wings over the face.

Janice whimpered. 'We've got to get the police! Oh, sorry Stella, you *are* the police. And we ought to tell the vicar. He's up the tower. Shall I go and fetch him?'

Stella firmly rejected this idea and told Janice to go and sit down and leave everything to her.

Janice went to flop onto her chair and watched, eyes staring, limbs beginning to shake uncontrollably with shock, as Stella took out her mobile phone and dialled. 'Guv. In the church... No... no... nothing missing. Something found. A body. A man. Been dead some hours, I'd say. Boxed up in the play chest. Head smashed in. Er... blunt force trauma to the head. Well, perhaps not 'blunt'? Too much blood for that. Sharp edge involved I think ... Ah, there it is... That figures... Murder weapon still at the scene...'

A rush of exclamations bursting from the superintendent interrupted her account, followed by a triumphant: 'Well, the info was spot on, then! She wasn't wrong, eh?'

'Sorry, sir? Who wasn't wrong?'

'Annyetta Barnsdale! That's the reason you're there on the spot, Constable. Information received. The lady rang in a couple of days back to tell us she'd found out her old man was planning a raid on the church. Going out on the job himself for once. She was on to me again a couple of hours ago, complaining that he hadn't come home last night. Spent the night in church, it seems. That'll be a first for Eddie... and the last.'

'She shopped him?'

'Traded. We prefer to say "traded". The lady was about to find herself in a bit of bother regarding possession of some property of highly dubious provenance. She came to realise - with a bit of encouragement - that her smartest move was to give us the goods on Eddie and throw herself on our mercy. But now she's unexpectedly a widow I think I'd better send someone along to the Moated Grange with a pair of handcuffs. Widows! They'll always bear watching!'

'Wait! Sir!' Stella yelled. 'A problem with that... I've never met the man Barnsdale but I'm pretty sure the man in the chest isn't *him.*' She quelled the spluttering at the other end by asking calmly: 'Why don't you take a look for yourself? Get this up on screen, sir.'

She switched on her phone camera and trailed it over the contents of the chest. The exclamations and questions came thick and fast as he received the images.

'But who in hell *is* that? Shift that white stuff out of the way, will you, and let's get a look at him! What a godawful mess! Show me that weapon again, Stella. What *is* that damned thing? Can you make it out?'

'Sir, may I remind you that your comments are being heard in church and that one of the lady churchwardens is right here with me at the moment. The object is, I believe, an ice-axe. It's tucked down the corpse's trousers with the head exposed... Yes, I do have some idea where it might have come from. And the deceased gentleman, on my first cursory viewing, I believe I can identify.'

'Deceased gentleman? Cursory viewing? Are you in a state of shock, Stella?'

A piercing wail cut into the increasingly edgy exchange. 'Why don't you s*ay* it? You *know* who it is! Look at the ring! On his right hand! And his hair! His lovely fair hair!' shrieked Janice. 'It's James! It's poor young James, isn't it?' She collapsed, sobbing noisily.

The ancient church clock gave a warning clunk and launched into its deafening hourly chime. Twelve interminable clangs sounded, anchoring Stella to the spot. At the last note, a shout of triumph and excitement rose up in the graveyard and outside, in the real world, the first bear flew past the window.

* * *

'Twenty minutes, sir?' Stella listened carefully to the spate of automatic instructions that flowed from her boss and when she could make herself heard again put in: 'Of course, Guv! Routine procedure. Got all that! But listen will you? There's a village jamboree going on in the churchyard. Children heavily involved. Hundreds of them in fact, swarming about flying their teddy bears... Yes, I said teddy bears. Yes, I said flying. Discretion the better part of reaction, do you think? Sensitive policing? Sir? No sirens? No flashing lights? Promise?'

DS Crackstone sighed. 'Cross my heart and hope to die,' he said drily.

He was as good as his word.

Between studying the corpse in a blend of revolted fascination and professional curiosity and comforting Janice, the twenty minutes sped by for Stella. But she greeted the large masculine presence of the superintendent with some relief as he slid tactfully through the door and down the aisle, placing his feet on the floorboards and avoiding the red wilton carpet. Crackstone acknowledged Janice with a nod and asked her to remain where she was. Plain clothes officers, he told Stella had been posted all around the site with instructions not to interfere with the jollifications outside which seemed, in fact, to be drawing to a close.

'The vicar was just announcing the winner,' he reported, cheerily. 'Heard him bellowing as I came up the path. After two disqualifications, it seems the honour goes to *Biggles.*' Talking to put Janice at her ease, Stella decided. *Establish a rapport. 'I may be the police but I'm human'*... First stage in interrogation...

'My men will be noting all names and addresses of attendees as they try to leave. They won't like it but they've had their fun... Scene of Crime Team on their way.' *Affirm power and efficiency.* The detective was rather bear-like himself, Stella thought: large, shambling, a superficial friendliness hiding his awful teeth and claws. 'Now then what have we got here? Come and tell me what makes you think this is the curate... God rest his soul,' he added awkwardly for form's sake.

Janice began to sob uncontrollably again.

* * *

It was an hour before Stella was dismissed to go home and leave the place clear for the SOCOs. She was asked to rejoin the team on site at three when Crackstone would take her with him to interview the treacherous Annyetta. As she closed the church door behind her, she was startled to be greeted by a lanky figure lounging on the wooden seat inside the porch.

''ere! Miss!' Liam Oxley claimed her attention.

'Liam! What on earth are you doing here? They should have shooed you off home!'

'They tried. I told them the blonde police officer needed to speak to me and they said it was all right to wait here so long as I didn't try to go inside... As if I would! What's up, then? Someone nicked the candlesticks?'

'None of your business. Watch the telly tonight. Local news after the football results. There's going to be a briefing. What do you want to see me for?'

He held out a grubby ten pound note. 'Winnings. Ten to one. And 'ere's the stake. He added a pound coin.

'You must have had a good day?'

'Brilliant!' To her surprise he spent the next five minutes outlining the betting patterns and the odds calculations with the detail and accuracy of a computer. Stella could barely follow. Curiosity pushed her to ask how he'd acquired this skill with numbers. 'From that new curate at the youth club,' he told her. 'Good bloke. Mathematician he says he used to be before 'e got God. Knows 'is stuff all right. Did you know 'ed done Vegas?'

He grinned and added: 'And I *mean* - done Vegas. Numbers is the key to the Universe, James says. Been showing us how to keep accounts ... so we'll know what's what when we go into business.' Stella fought back a shudder at the spectre of Liam in business and listened on with silent encouragement. A smile of sly pride softened his sharp features. 'But I think I've been able to give 'im a few pointers!'

She waited for him to enlarge on this but he seemed to think he'd said enough and got to his feet, adjusting his cap to a more rakish angle.

'Well, thanks for this,' she said, waving the ten pound note. 'I think I'll donate it to the church roof fund.'

Liam grunted. 'Waste of cash! Might as well chuck it down a drain. You could get a case of beer for that!'

* * *

Under her mother's gentle interrogation, cup of tea in hand, DC Kenton sketched in her eventful morning.

'But you're not telling me someone persuaded James to step into the chest and lie still while they bashed his head in, are you? Even at gun point - and I assume frightful old Barnsdale would have been armed - I can't see athletic young James just meekly doing as he was told... no... there'd have been signs of a struggle.' She looked questioningly at her daughter.

'You're right. He wasn't killed in the chest. There were drag marks on the carpet. While I was waiting for the cavalry to arrive I tracked them back. All the way to the vestry. That's where they'll find their killing scene. The chest was just what they'll call the deposition spot.'

'The ice axe. He kept all his equipment in there. It was never locked.'

'Yes. I poked about a bit. Lifted a hanging on the south wall - a hanging that hadn't been there before. Blood spatter pattern behind it. The first blow probably. It took several to kill him I think. He was probably still breathing when they put him into the chest because the blood continued to flow. Someone had unrolled a waterproof ground sheet and manoeuvred his body onto it, dragged it to the chest and heaved it in. Someone strong. Or two or three people. The sheet was folded up and stashed away behind the chest.'

'They'd tidied up to gain time? It wouldn't have been discovered until Monday morning at the earliest if you and Janice hadn't been poking about. I wonder whatever possessed her to go in on a Saturday morning? Wednesday was her next duty day. Lurking about to catch a glimpse of James, I suppose... Another one of those! Anyway... hiding the corpse was probably intended to give whoever it was a whole weekend to get away.'

'But the weirdest thing, Mum, was the wings. You know - from the nativity play - the angel's wings. His face was covered over by two carefully placed wings.'

'I can help you there!' Mrs Kenton was pleased to announce. 'I've seen that on *Criminal Minds*. Covering up the features is a sign that the killer knows his victim. It's a mark of respect or remorse.'

'Rubbish!' said Stella. 'That's not how we do policing in Cambridge.'

'I know! You're not encouraged to think outside the box! Just put a tick in it and move on to the next,' scoffed Mrs Kenton. 'Watch your back, don't stick your neck out and keep your brain out of gear! Listen Stella: one alert brain at the scene is worth more than any amount of vacuum-bag and test-tube evidence. I bet I could work this out in five minutes, sitting here at the kitchen table if I had the facts before me.' She looked speculatively at Stella. 'Now go through that again slowly.

'It wasn't Eddie Barnsdale, you know,' Mrs Kenton decided. 'He'd met poor James - once - but I can't see him bothering to put feathers over his face. And why would he waste time lugging him down the aisle and heaving him into the play chest? He'd have left the body in the vestry and done a bunk.'

Stella gave this theory her consideration. 'If Annyetta is to be believed, then Eddie was out and about and in the church last night. With or without accomplices - we don't know yet. Not planning on a murder - perhaps the curate was hiding in the vestry in anticipation of the burglary, jumped out and shouted "boo" just as he was getting going. Startled, in the dark, Eddie lost it, picked up and used the nearest implement to hand. If he'd kept a cool head, he *would* have hidden the body somewhere less public - the vestry was always open... people in and out all the time. The keys to the tower were kept in there and tourists always asked to climb up for the view at weekends. Putting the body in the chest gave him the hours he needed to get away.'

'I'm not convinced. Oh, I agree about the playing for time. It was a good place - it was the *only* place where no one would look for some time... In fact not until the Monday morning play group came rioting in... Perhaps someone knew all this... I mean was familiar with the routine. And the killing? Violent, passionate... an outburst instantly regretted? An attempt at atonement by the careful laying out in the box. And the angel's wings? Creepy!'

'I see where you're going with this, Mum.' Stella was subdued and wary, not wanting to follow where her mother was leading. But she added: 'And the ice axe? Did I tell you? It was... sort of... displayed. Not hidden. Not chucked into the river or the bushes. It was tucked neatly into his belt. Just about where he would have worn it had he been climbing. A gift to the inspecting officer? Felt like it!'

'Someone saying: "Look, I may have murdered him but

I'm not trying to hide it." Someone who knew the church, knew James, had some personal feelings for him, regretted his action and needed a day or two to complete his arrangements.'

'You're saying "he, his" Mum. Had you considered that it might have been a woman?'

'Oh yes,' said Mrs Kenton quietly. 'James passed through this village like a shooting star. Never seen anything like him before. He turned all heads and captured some hearts, I do believe.'

'Girl friends?'

'None known. Certainly no local attachments. He was always very... correct. Friendly but with the protective force-field of the dog collar always in place. Like the Rev Blandish he always favoured traditional church gear.'

Stella grunted. 'Some women see that as a magnet... an alluring challenge. Even Annyetta Barnsdale seemed to fancy her chances according to the Guv. But could a woman have got him into the box?'

'Oh, yes, I think so. It's the adrenaline. In extremis, even the feeblest people can move weights you wouldn't credit.... That was on *Crime Insight,*' she added apologetically. 'And have you ever seen Mrs Barnsdale? You can forget about all that lily on the brow and fading roses on the cheeks stuff - she's built like Boudica of the Iceni!'

Stella's phone rang and her mother made no attempt to move out of earshot.

'That was the Super - as you probably heard. They've got him! Eddie Barnsdale! Climbing into a first class carriage on the Eurostar at St Pancras. They had to arrest him to get him back to Cambridge. He denies all knowledge. Never went near the church. Claims he was leaving Annyetta and getting away to a new life in Spain. Doing it on the quiet because he was keen - considering the divorce which now seems inevitable - to keep from her any knowledge of the bank accounts he's got in place against just such an emergency. The Guv wants me to go back in and help him interview a very angry Annyetta in her gracious home.' She glanced at her watch. 'I've got an hour. Time for another cup of tea.'

* * *

The banging on the door was urgent.

'Can you squeeze another cup out of the pot, Stella?' her mother asked hesitantly. 'Um... here's young Liam with something to say to you. Sit down will you, love?'

Liam, eyes swivelling round the cheerful kitchen, grunted a refusal of tea, took a quick swig of his Red Bull and launched straight into his account.

'Just been listening to local radio. He's dead, i'nee? James. Smashed up with 'is own ice-axe. Did they get that right?'

Stella noticed that the pale face was troubled, the sharp eyes swimming with distress and pleading with her to tell him he'd got it wrong. Sadly, she confirmed the radio report, careful not to give away further information.

Liam gulped and covered his face with his hands. When he looked at her again, the little boy she had just glimpsed was gone, the severe features were set with purpose, the head tilted defiantly. Even his voice had changed. He was speaking slowly and carefully, the deliberate sloppiness discarded. 'He never deserved that. Good bloke. Too good! I warned him to keep his trap shut!'

'Liam? If there's something you know that...'

Liam shot to his feet. 'You bet there's something I know! Can you get me into the church with that card of yours? Good. There's something you ought to take a look at. I think I can show you what got him killed.'

* * *

The crime team greeted Stella with easy familiarity and waved her through with her 'material witness' as she decided to call Liam. It was more tricky to run the gauntlet of the double act of her superintendent and the Revered Blandish, neither of whom seemed to relish the presence of the youth under the hallowed roof. The vicar frowned and seemed on the point of questioning the boy further but Liam removed his cap, stood tall and glowered up defiantly at the pair of them. Stella was impressed by the boy's courage. The policeman and the vicar were imposing figures. Tall men in suits, figures of authority and on their own patch.

'Finished in the vestry have they?' Stella asked hurriedly. 'Good. We're just going to poke our noses round the door. There's something Liam wants me to take a look at. Okay with you, sir?'

'Yes. If you have to. You'll have to manage without me for a few minutes... the vicar's just about to show me up the bell tower. Four storeys high, I'm assured! Good view of access and escape routes for heavy vehicles from up there. Round the back, by way of Glebe Meadow. Be down in a minute. Don't disturb the...' Frozen by Stella's raised eyebrow, he hurried off in pursuit of the vicar who was already springing up the twisting steps leading to the tower. She heard the stairs creak under the weight of the super's bear-like frame as he climbed after him.

Liam flinched at the sight of the blood spatter on the whitewashed wall and refused to go into the room. He directed Stella to a book shelf mounted over the desk. 'That big blue leather-backed one on the right,' he told her.

She took down the volume. 'Church accounts? This what you meant, Liam?'

'That's right. James was showing us the layout. Before he got us on to spreadsheets, he thought we ought to see how it used to be done in the days of the dinosaurs. Still is round 'ere.' He sniffed his scorn for all things ecclesiastical. 'He sat down there at the desk and showed us. Me and Danny. Didn't take long to get the idea... And then he shut up. Just like that. Forgot we were with him, I think. Started turning the pages forward and back, forward and back. Muttering. Got his calculator out and did a bit of flashy stuff. He looked at me and he could tell I knew. Danny didn't cotton on. I kept schtum. Made nothing of it.'

Stella was leaping ahead of him. Lowering her voice she asked: 'But you made it your business to find out, didn't you, Liam? Came back again after hours and took a sneaky look? It's easy enough to get into here.'

'Old grandpa Wilkins keeps his key in his outhouse.' Liam shrugged. 'Everybody knows that.'

'And what did you find?' Stella could hardly breathe but she managed to keep her voice level.

'Persistent and heavy misappropriation of church funds,' he said succinctly, in a tone disturbingly like the dead curate's. 'It took me longer than James to figure it out because the Rev's no muppet and he'd hidden it deep. It'd been going on for a long time. Steady drip not a rush... That old Dodo's been having it away with the village's cash for decades. God knows where it goes!' He gave a snort of unholy amusement at his unwitting insight.

'God - and now Liam?' Stella suggested.

'Plenty of cash coming in. Always something or other to save up for. Always people ready to sponsor others to do daft things to raise it. Did you know James canoed seventeen times up and down the Cam last year?' He added savagely: 'Nearly done himself in! And for what? That must have bought at least three tyres for the vicar's new Range Rover. Seen it parked in the vicarage drive? I wonder if he'll point *that* out to your boss from the top of the tower? Says 'es got private means... yer - very private!'

They looked at each other in horror. 'Liam - what are we saying?'

'That your boss is up there, four storeys high with a killer. James had it out with him last night and the old geezer let rip and bashed him with his own ice axe to shut him up. He knew what I was going to show you. He knows he's had it. Only one way down from there. Better go to the bottom of the steps and grab him.' He grinned a wolf's grin. 'Never seen an arrest before. Got some hand cuffs have you in your Gucci bag?'

Stella was already tearing down the nave, shouting her boss's name. She screamed as a dark form dropped silently past the clerestory window. She gasped as a dull thump announced a deadly landing.

She and Liam were still standing rigidly by the stairs when Superintendent Crackstone charged down dangerously fast, ashen-faced, clutching an envelope and choking with emotion. 'Did you see...? Shoved this at me and chucked himself over! Before I could move! He was there one minute and gone the next! Why in hell...?'

'I expect it's all in the envelope, sir. Suicide. I think he set you up as a witness. So that no one else was involved. All planned. Nothing you could do.' She'd never seen her boss so distraught. On impulse she put a comforting arm around his shoulders. Liam fished a can from a pocket of his droopy cargoes and thrust it at him. To his credit, the Super rejected neither gesture. He tolerated Stella's swiftly regretted hug, tore the can open and took a glug. He grimaced, checked what he was drinking and took another glug. 'Probably all for the best, sir. Shall I come with you to have a look at him? And then you'd better hear what Liam has to say.'

* * *

'He never meant it to be covered up. Weapon on display,

and suicide planned. He wrote a note for the boss apologising for what he called "the inconvenience",' Stella explained to her mother.

'There was more to it than just the shame of being discovered up to his armpits in the cash drawer though.' Mrs Kenton was not yet satisfied. 'You don't know the half of it, Liam! Have another brownie, love... The wings? Does Liam know about the wings? Well, I don't think he spread them over his face as a mark of respect... He couldn't bear to look at his face. Even dead. Never could, you know, when the poor chap was alive. Eyes always slid sideways, along with his sarcastic comments. He hated him. Hated his good looks, his popularity with the young people in the village - well with *everyone* in the village. James was a difficult man to stand next to. He made everyone look less than they were, if you know what I mean... I think rage and jealousy just boiled over. But, being a religious man by training at least, he didn't try to hide his act of murder.'

'But he *did* Mrs Kenton," Liam pointed out. "If he meant to turn himself in or top himself, why did he bother to put him in the chest over the weekend? It's not as if he was doing a runner,' he asked.

'He wanted to fly the Teddy Bears!' said Stella with sudden insight. 'It was planned. It was *his* thing not James's. Something his curate hadn't yet charmed away from him. It had to go ahead. He wanted the children to remember him as the genial joker who launched their toys from the tower. A last flourish. A farewell to the village.'

'An inside job, you could call it,' said Mrs Kenton. 'And there you were putting your money on old Barnsdale, Stella!'

'Naw! She never! Constable's too smart to bet on the favourite,' said Liam sagely.

A Dark Issue

A Hallowe'en story

Cambridge. Late October.

A young woman lingered by the notice board at the gate of All Hallows Church, clearly looking for something. It wasn't easy to find a single hand-written sheet amongst the overabundance of junk screaming for the visitor's attention.

Here were the usual invitations to enter the church, trailing enticements such as: the thigh bone of St Eustache, cruelly martyred, a page from the prayer book of Queen Isabella and an oak lectern once pounded by the fist of a dissenting preacher. These and other stranger delights were advertised, fighting for attention with the dozens of polythene-wrapped flyers stuck on the railings, luring passers-by to attend concerts, plays and flower festivals in the city.

These eyesores were ignored by the solitary young woman huddled in the scarf. She was perfectly dressed for this sun-filled late-autumn day in khaki trousers and boots, black leather jacket and white blouse; her fair hair was gathered unfussily into a classic knot at the back of her neck. A tourist perhaps? Scandinavian? Northern Italian? The sunglasses pushed casually up onto her head suggested that, and the tourist guide to the city she held with a finger marking her place confirmed it. A very close observer might have noticed which of the printed sheets (not prominently displayed) had finally caught her attention and, looking over her shoulder, might have read:

8 p.m. Friday, October 31ˢᵗ
Goth Vespers.
Music in a minor key.
Discussion of the dark issues
of modern life:
* Distrust
* Depression
* Death

She made no note, simply looked with rather more absorption than might have been expected. It would have been harder to imagine anyone less Gothic in appearance than this young woman.

Stella Kenton was, in spite of her sleek blonde cosmopolitan looks, a Cambridge girl. Born in the Rosie Maternity and educated at a city school, she had been a policewoman for six years and had worked her way up into the detective branch. But today she was off duty and the impulse to examine discreetly the Church and its connection with the Goth cult was an entirely personal one. A family one. Her little cousin Lily was a Goth. She'd always been different. The problem child of a broken home. Stella had tried her best to care for and befriend her, to keep her anchored in the family but Lily had grown into a defiant and awkward teenager. She'd chosen an alternative life-style and her constant sneering at Stella's orthodox job had led to an irreconcilable rift. Goth and cop - they had nothing in common. Since Lily had declared herself, dyed her hair black and taken to wearing weird white make-up, floating black clothes and only coming out after dark, all contact had been lost.

Until yesterday.

With another shiver, Stella turned her back on the dark

border of evergreen foliage that encircled the ancient stones in a livid noose and headed off, as everyone did, for the sunlit bustle of King's Parade. She decided to brave the chill of October, and sat down at a café table outside on the pavement, her spirits lifted by the sight of England's most magnificent chestnut tree standing sentinel beside the soaring Tudor façade of King's College Chapel.

By some meteorological alchemy, the skies over Cambridge took on an intense Provençal blue in October, offering a glowing background to the upward-thrusting, spirit-lifting architecture. Here was a priceless page from a medieval Book of Hours to be wondered at and enjoyed. And all for the price of an espresso.

Stella tore her eyes from the view and took her cousin's note from her bag. She read it again, making a little more sense of it now she'd seen the church.

The writing was the scrawl of one who'd never bothered to practice. Lily's fingers whizzed along a keyboard but rarely put pen to paper. It had been pushed by hand - after dark of course - through her letter box four days before. Untraceable. Not even signed. At least not signed with her real name. And yet Lily had clearly intended to declare her identity. Once, as a small child, Lily had provoked the older girl beyond reason and Stella had snapped. She'd rounded on her. '*Lily*? Whoever thought *that* a good name for a fiend like you? Lilies are pure and elegant and good! They should have called you Lilith!'

Stella had instantly regretted her outburst but the child appeared pleased to have annoyed her and also - intrigued. 'Lilith? Who's she then? One of your Greek goddesses?' she'd sneered.

'No. She was the Queen of Hell. In Ancient Middle Eastern mythology.'

Lily had considered this for a moment with a sly smile and tasted the name on her tongue, repeating: 'Lilith' as though charmed.

Stella had hoped the insult had been forgotten but, years later, it was surfacing again.

No address. No date. In hopeless, uncaring lettering she read:

S. Sinking too far, too fast. Any chance of a life-belt? All Hallows. 8pm next Friday.

And, at the end, simply: *Queen of Hell.*

Stella remembered.

And here she was, looking about her. Half an hour's reconnaissance prevented a fortnight's muddle, she'd always found. But why would a simple evening service in a city-centre church strike such dread into Lily that she would ask her despised cousin for help after all these years? Dark Issues? Was it wise to open up dark issues for inspection on this particular day? Hallowe'en at the church of All Hallows being celebrated after dark by a congregation of black-clothed Goths? This sounded to Stella like deliberate sensation-seeking. Unhealthy.

She opened up the guide to the occult she'd found on a book-stall in the market and looked up Hallowe'en. Or *'Samhain'*. She rather thought this particular congregation would choose to use the Celtic word. The very ancient pagan festival had been taken over by the Romans who'd gone in for apple-bobbing and harvest feasting in a jolly way, then medieval Christians who'd turned it into a more prayer-full occasion to celebrate the soul: 'All Hallows' Eve', and latterly by trick-or-treating Americans, each succeeding culture taming and sweetening the harsh original.

But all agreed: this was the day in the year when spirits walked.

The veil that separated the living from the dead grew thin on the last day of October and the dead were able to take on their human shape once more, slip through and communicate. Stella took a deep breath and closed the book. If spirits were going to break through the veil, then they might well make the attempt at the church of All Hallows where she reckoned the defences were weak. A rational girl, she didn't believe ghosts led a separate existence. Ghosts were a creation of the human mind. Vivid enough to the people who experienced them perhaps but no more real than a daydream or a nightmare.

But then the doubt sneaked in - what if she were wrong? What if the spirits of the dead did lead a detached existence?

Supposing they existed and were eager to find their way through, she could think of no better worm-hole through time and into a receptive brain than this darkly atmospheric place. Like a rotten tooth, it still had its roots and nerve connections to a deep past beyond and below the present church. And if a child of light and science like herself could be unnerved by it, what might it do to a company of seekers after the dark who were already pre-disposed to glory in the occult?

Lily had always been fragile, impressionable, yearning after something just out of reach. Vulnerable to anyone who promised to supply what she thought she needed: tattoos, drugs, emotional support. And yes - excitement. Lily had always scripted dramas for herself and played the part of Queen. But never before had she asked for help. Something in her life must have gone terribly wrong.

Stella picked up her bag and set off to police headquarters. She'd just make it back for the 11.00 a.m. Mid Week Meeting in the Muster Room if she got a move on.

*

The other detectives, all ranks, were slouching about

looking in a marked manner at their watches and muttering. 'Waste of time... I've got forms to process... Witnesses to nail... Who the hell's he think he is?'

'He's Supercop, that's who. Deal with it and move on!' Stella heard the girly voice of the lowest-ranking female officer chirp up. She shut her mouth but was too late to avoid becoming the target of everyone's bad humour. She bustled over to the coffee machine, still babbling. 'He likes to see the whites of our eyes. Face to face contact. Builds trust, you know. Churchill... Napoleon... Ross Kemp - they all like to be seen mucking in with the lower ranks.'

A pair of blood-shot eyes forced themselves open and Detective Inspector Fielding, Stella's immediate superior, roused himself to cover her back.Yet again. 'She's right. Just because she's got a degree in Psychology doesn't mean she's always wrong. They've done it for Education - revived the three 'R's and stuck an Afghan War vet in every classroom. Superheads parachuted in from Lord knows where... They've done it to the Banks. Only a matter of time before they got around to Law Enforcement. And now we've got our very own Supercop. Could be worse - he could have been flown in from Chicago.'

'*Yorkshire*, though?' someone protested. 'What insight can that piece of millstone grit have into a place like Cambridge?'

'A good question, D.C. Smithson,' a smooth voice purred from the doorway. 'And you're not the first one to ask it. What's the relationship between distance and civilisation? Are they inversely proportional? My hero, the Reverend Sidney Smith, on being sent out from Mayfair to run a parish in wildest Yorkshire,' the newcomer went on in an engagingly chatty tone while making his way over to the front of the gathering, 'that is Hull, in... what was it?... 1809 or thereabouts... declared that his new living was so far out of the way, it was eleven miles from a lemon.'

County Commander Loxley smiled benignly at the company. 'No shortage of lemons down here, I see.'

He caught sight of Stella, mug in hand, at the drinks machine. 'Or of the brew that cheers. Bring me one over, constable.'

A silence fell. Everyone knew that Stella hated to be expected to serve the coffee. She'd been the moving force behind the acquisition of the gleaming piece of Italian engineering but she refused to service it or the slobs who left their mugs lying about growing mould. They grinned and waited to see what she'd do.

'Right away, Commander.' The warm voice, the smooth blonde bob and slim figure would have done credit to an air hostess. She oozed over and handed it to him. 'You'll find it's just what you need,' she added with her best hand-maiden's intonation.

His attention on his audience, Loxley took the mug with a casual nod of thanks in her direction. Realising that all eyes were suddenly on him, he took a sip and manfully kept his craggy features in control as the black, sugarless espresso hit him. He even took a deep breath and sipped again. 'Nothing like a good Italian,' he muttered. 'To get you going in the morning.

'Now, I won't keep you from your busy schedule. I've posted this week's bulletin on your internal mail and you can scroll through it at your leisure - if you have any. I wanted to see you all, literally for just that. I need to cast an eye over you. Something a bit unusual's come up and I want a volunteer for some undercover work in the city. Don't all rush. This volunteer we will now arrive at by self-elimination. Just so no one accuses me of victimisation or favouritism. Gather into a group in the middle, will you.'

He waited until everyone had shuffled grudgingly into a scrum.

'Come on, play nicely, Sinclair! Now - go over to the side if you judge that you fill the following descriptions: One - All those carrying over a stone excess weight... Off you go.'

A shamingly large number of the men sucked in their beer-guts and shambled off to the side.

'Those over five-foot ten - disappear.'

Stella was left in the centre with two other women and four senior male detectives.

'All those over thirty - goodbye.'

She found herself standing alone.

'Well, well. What are we left with?' He seemed pleased with himself.

'The number you first thought of, sir?'

He gave her a very sharp look. 'You'll do. D. C. Kenton isn't it? Sally? Sorry - Stella. Report to me in my office at four o'clock.'

'That's not right, Stella!' D.C. Smithson sought her out to protest the moment Loxley left the room. 'He can't make you volunteer! Where does he think he is? In the trenches? "Now who'd like to go over the top?" Inappropriate behaviour. Abuse of rank. Tell your union. And how did he know our names?'

'That man knows everybody's name, Eddie. And their waist measurement and shoe size. It's called Man-Management - he's been on a course.'

'Ah! That'll be Judicious Exploitation of Human Resources.' Smithson was a stickler for detail.

'Nah! That's CRAP. Calculated Re-use of Available Personnel, Ed. And I think he *wrote* the course.'

*

When Stella entered his office, Loxley was busying himself at a tray, capable hands conjuring two drinks from bags, filters, bowls and jugs. Finally happy with his production, he handed her a black coffee, his eyebrow only slightly raised, and held up his own mug. 'Tea. Milk. Two sugars. For future reference.'

She nodded and hurriedly changed the subject. 'Why me, sir? How can I help?'

He peered at her and grimaced. 'Now I see you up close... I may have made a mistake. Colouring's all wrong. You're very well-scrubbed. I need someone to do a bit of infiltrating for me. Constable, what do you know about underground groups in the city - Punks, Goths, Vampires... that sort of thing? Are you aware of a presence?'

'Punks died out a long time ago. Vampires are very last year. Neo-lycanthropes? We're strong on them at the moment.'

'Eh? Come again, Constable...'

'Shape-Shifters. There's a few wannabee-werewolves who gather on Midsummer Common in silver collars to bay at the full moon.'

'Do they give us any trouble?'

'Not much. They get drunk and chuck a few beer cans about.'

'Wouldn't get my juices flowing,' he commented.

'They spark it up a bit, sir. They wear hairy jerkins and leather trousers and establish precedence in the pack by competing to see which one of them can pee the highest against that chestnut tree in the middle of the Common. The others then offer him their necks to bite as a sign of subjection. And then the ceremonial howling starts.'

He swallowed and scratched a note on a pad. 'Nothing like this in Yorkshire. And we have the moors for it. Ecological damage, grievous bodily harm, noise pollution. And the alpha-male du jour? Are we aware...?'

'Oh, yes. The highest achiever for the last three months

running has been one Rufus Fleshrender, aka Gareth Green from Godmanchester. It's all on file.'

'Clown!' he exclaimed, making a further note.

'Not at all, sir. Gareth has a degree in Ancient History and a part-time job with the University Library.'

Loxley gave her a hopeless stare. 'Not sure whether to nick them for littering or pass round the hat at the monthly performance.'

'Pack gatherings fall off after Hallowe'en when the cold nights come. You won't be bothered by them until next April.'

'How do we come by this information, Constable?' he asked shrewdly.

'Er...' This man was punctilious. He would check. 'We've got into the pack, sir. Gareth Green is one of ours. He's a Special Constable.'

'Very special if he's undercover, dabbling in the occult and bringing the human race into disrepute.' Supercop was not pleased.

He put down his pen, looking thoughtful. 'And it's three months our Gareth has held throat-tearing rights over his fellow roughs, you say? Clearly enjoying himself too much. I'll redeploy him. Well, you'll be glad to hear that your own target is far less challenging. No biting, no baying, no peeing involved but - blood? - there may be blood.'

He had her whole attention.

'It's *Goths.* Ever heard of Goths, Constable?'

'Goths?' This was a surprise. 'They pop in and out of fashion. In at the moment. They're secretive but non-violent, on the young side, seem only to come out after dark and are never a problem as far as the police are concerned.'

Loxley nodded.

'Agreed, constable. Not a problem for us. Gentle souls, you'd say, on the side of the angels, searching for the truth. Just like me. It's not as though I were asking you to infiltrate a militant bunch. Like the Grind-the-Government Group, the Bash-a Banker Brigade or the Angry Anarchists. If this mob made you a Molotov Cocktail they'd pop an olive in it.'

'Sir,' Stella decided to own to an interest before he took things further. 'You ought to know - my young cousin's one. A Goth. For the last five years - since she was fourteen. We haven't spoken for a long time. She dropped out of life a while back and that included *my* life. Cops and Goths, they don't mix. But I'm sure I could contact her again and...'

'Blow whatever cover you've got? No, leave it until you hear what's going on. In the centre of civilised Cambridge. A lemon's throw away from the Market Square.'

He passed across the desk a handbill very like the one she'd seen before.

Church of All Hallows'
Friday 31ˢᵗ October
GOTH EUCARIST
8.p.m.
Music.
Followed by discussion of dark issues:
Distrust,
Depression,
Death.

She noted that in this copy someone had drawn a circle in red ink around the third dark issue, adding the artistic touch of a drop of blood poised to drip from the foot of the letter 'h' of 'Death'.

'Very nice, sir. Just what Goths appreciate. Their kind of music, followed by their kind of conversation. Dark issues are what get them going. It's good to see someone's offered them a forum... a safe meeting place where they can indulge in a bit of group therapy. With an earnest young priest to lead the discussion, I expect. Giving them a gentle push towards the path of light. They can see that they're not alone in their troubles. I'm all in favour.'

'So am I. A bit of soul-poaching is none of my business. But if anyone lays his mitts on the church silver, I'll 'ave 'im!'

'This hints at much worse than metal theft. Death? Murder even?'

'Possible. And I can think of more auspicious days in the calendar than All Hallows' Eve to have their gathering, perhaps... Remind me, Kenton, what the significance of this particular evening is.'

She was sure he knew and wouldn't appreciate a lengthy answer. She remembered her cousin Lily's eager and rather desperate attempts to explain her new enthusiasm and summarised: 'It's of Celtic origin. *Samhain*. It's the night of the year when the veil between the world of the living and the afterworld of the ancestors grows thinnest. So thin that occasionally the spirits of the dead slip through and walk alongside the living. To pass on messages or right wrongs.'

Loxley snorted. 'What? Like "Remember to pay the gas bill" or "The diamond ring should have gone to Gladys"?'

'Yes. It's a powerful belief and it seems to be ingrained in most people's natures, even though it's been reduced to trick-or-treating spookiness by Hollywood directors and chocolate manufacturers. I must say I wouldn't fancy that time or that place to hob-nob with a bunch of black-robed depressive characters.'

'Exactly. I went round there myself to take a look,' he said.

Rumour had it that the new broom had been spotted sweeping in some strange corners of the town. And Rumour, for once, it seemed was right.

'Terrible place! I'm not exactly sensitive to atmosphere

created by architecture and vegetation but by heck, that little pile of medieval witchery gave me the creeps! Damp old stones huddling inside a ring of rotting livid green laurels and spiky underbrush. There could be a corpse or two, the rotting bones of Shergar or the Gateway to Hell hidden under there and we'd never know.'

Stella smiled, amused to find his reaction had been much the same as hers. 'And the interior, sir? Did you...?'

'Worse! If you weren't depressed when you went in, you would be by the time you came out. Do you know what they've stuck in there to tempt the tourist? Some martyr's thigh bone - who the devil's Eustache when he's at home? - a mouldering page from a hymn book and a stained witch bottle with something gloopy in the bottom. "Aha!" I thought when I saw *that* little offering, "Something's crawled in there and died." But I was wrong. It contained the quartered and burned entrails of the Earl of Chesterton. A local hero, I was informed by the young priest who came to hover at my elbow. The Earl wasn't a hero to his monarch, Elizabeth, apparently. She had him executed for treason and dabbling in the Black Arts. And some fan scooped up and bottled the left-overs.'

The commander chuckled nastily. 'Wouldn't you just like to hand that mess to Forensics and see their little faces crumple!'

'There was no priest in evidence when I was there early this morning.'

Loxley narrowed his eyes and swigged his tea. 'Well, *you* look like an innocent tourist - not like someone who's casing the joint for precious metals. Now, a big bloke like me in a donkey jacket gets the instant priestly presence, the hand under the elbow and the firm, "May I help you, sir?"' Thoughtful for a moment, he added: 'Stout feller, though. *I* wouldn't challenge an ugly bruiser like me, even in God's house. Anyway - mental alarms had clearly been triggered. And so they should! Silver, copper and brass everywhere and much of it not even nailed down! Door left unlocked. Copies of keys unaccounted for... The Reverend Sweetman and I introduced ourselves, checked credentials and had a friendly chat. He's new in the job and has a few concerns about the church himself. Interesting...' Then, shrewdly and abruptly: 'Are you going to tell me what's all this to you, Constable?'

Stella placed her cousin's note on the desk with a brief explanation.

'Your cousin's mixed up with this bunch of heathens?'

'I'm not condemning them, sir. I've said - they're never a problem for us. And the Cambridge chapter have something of a reputation. Intellectual. Few in number. Young. Tend to come out after dark, commune with like-minded souls and go home quietly to watch *Nosferatu* for the tenth time.'

'Right, I get it. Opera cape rather than monk's habit... *Mysteries of Udolpho* rather than *Revelations of a Teenage Vampyre*... But whoever this is seems - unusually - to be trying to attract the attention of the Law. They've let us have both barrels. A cry for help, are we hearing?'

'A cry you're going to answer, sir?'

'Of course. This is the new policing. My officers don't stand back and watch and film and consult the CCTV then slap the cuffs on weeks later. They get in first and prevent. Oh, I know it's not sexy! *Possible murder averted,* as a headline, doesn't pack the same punch as *Butchered corpse of blonde model found in undergrowth.* But to hell with the scandal sheets! This is most probably a hoax but I'm taking no chances. And I'm sure you want to do whatever you can to straighten out your little cousin.'

His sudden smile was beatific, involving, hard to resist. A man eager for challenges and full of energy. 'Right then, it's a date. All Hallows on Friday evening. Sorry it's not Carluccio's. Got anything planned? Can you do Gothic? Dirty yourself up a bit? How do you fancy a little Trick-

or-Treating, Constable?'

*

Loxley managed not to scream when she entered his office at seven on the eve of All Hallows but the gasp and the double-take and the: "By Gow! Who let the bats out?" were very satisfying. Stella couldn't blame him - she'd frightened herself when she'd passed a shop window on the way in. Dyed black hair, white face, dark red lipstick, a long black skirt and evening cape. And under the Hallowe'en fantasy a pair of flat-heeled boots she could kick out or run fast in.

'I parked the broomstick at the door,' she said. 'This what you had in mind, sir?'

'Morticia's evil little sister, I presume? You're channelling the Adams family?' He seemed disconcerted and Stella wondered whether she'd oversteered. 'Er... is this... er... process reversible?' he asked.

'The hair dye is only semi-permanent, henna tattoos and make-up come straight off. The kit is all borrowed from my granny. No face furniture. Goths don't go in for that stuff.'

'Well, in a town full of students, you're going to blend right in tonight. Good luck with it. Just keep an eye out and report back. Got your phone hidden under all that? Good. It's probably a load of cobblers and if anyone drops down dead tonight it'll be through boredom. The most you can hope for is to collar some joker for wasting police time. Have a nice evening!'

*

Stella turned away from the brightly-lit hubbub of the Market Square and made her way reluctantly down Benedict's Alley into the square in front of All Hallows'

Church. One feeble old-fashioned lamp shone out from a corner, exaggerating the gloom, deepening the shadows rather than dispelling them. Three cloaked figures had gathered beneath the lamp, clinging to the last available light before detaching themselves and moving off as a group down the paved path to the church.

She hung back, nervous but determined, fear driven out for the moment by the invigorating rush of energy a new job always brought. She stayed alert to her surroundings, waiting to see who was arriving and what the groupings were. A pair of shadows drifted silently past her, followed by two more pairs, another group of three and, she was relieved to notice, four people who entered one at a time. She wouldn't then stand out when she made her solo entrance. Stella was looking out for her cousin but acknowledged that after all these years she might not recognise the grown-up Lily even without the disguise of the Goth robes she'd be wearing. A carefully timed ten minutes before the start of the service, Stella slipped into the church.

*

Soft candle-light, a trace of incense, and playing quietly in the background, a romantic string piece. After a few bars she recognised the melancholy conversation between the two violins of Bach's concerto in D minor. The Reverend Sweetman, grey-clad like the congregation, was officiating at the altar, busily doing what priests do in the minutes before the performance starts. He turned to assess the size of the audience and remembered just in time to suppress the automatic smile of welcome that had been about to enliven his attractive face.

The nave was surprisingly full.

Most of the pews were occupied and Stella hesitated, seeking out a seat strategically placed for observation and easy exit at the rear. The priest caught her eye and beckoned her to move forward, mouthing the words: 'Empty pew over here, Miss!'

In the crowd, he hadn't noticed the man already sitting at the far side of the pew with his back to the church wall. Stella respected the occupant's solitary state, nodded politely and placed herself in the centre of the space, leaving three feet between them. He did not acknowledge her, remaining motionless, hooded head lowered as if in prayer. Most of the congregation were wearing hoods she noted, though some of the girls were bareheaded, flaunting spectacular hairdos. And not one resembled her cousin.

The violins sobbed together and spiralled off to a vanishing point in harmonious melancholy just as the great bell on the tower struck the first of eight notes. Stella noted the careful stage management. On the seventh stroke the priest held up his hands to indicate he was about to address the group. On the eighth stroke a shift of air down the aisle behind Stella announced the entrance of a latecomer. Primed for his start, the priest appeared not to notice.

Black-cloaked but not hooded, a dark-haired girl settled down soundlessly at Stella's side, looking neither to right nor left. With an effort, Stella managed not to cry out: 'Lily!' Her arms ached to reach out and fold her cousin in a hug but she remembered that distrust, depression and death were on the menu and whoops of joy would be out of place. She was so disturbed by what a sideways discreet examination of her cousin's face revealed, she heard little of the priest's opening speech.

Lily was ill.

It was hard to be certain when white make-up and kohl-lined eyes were the order of the day but the girl's face had the thin, grey transparency of petals left to rot on a grave. Wrinkled and insubstantial. Old beyond her years.

When she reached out to pick up one of the prayer books that had been laid out along the ledge in front of them, the sleeve of her gown slipped back revealing bruises and traces of cuts.

Stella longed for the whole pantomime to be over. Surely one entered a church or temple of any religion to hear messages of hope, salvation, forgiveness, good intentions? The mood of gloom and the yearning of this crowd to experience nothing more than a reflection of their own negative feelings mocked the setting and seemed to be taxing the priest's capacity. His curly red hair flared like a welcoming beacon, optimism threatened to break out in his tone of voice and the corners of his mouth twitched with the effort of suppressing a smile.

He had kicked off with a discussion of depression making references to the advances of science and medicine in the field. Words such as: understanding, analysis, therapy, love, hope, would keep surfacing in his talk.

This was not going down well.

His audience of angst-ridden souls fidgeted. One or two voices joined in the talk, cutting through the easy optimism with a querulous or assertive recitation of personal experiences with no attempt to sustain a consistent or objective view. Realising that the meeting was too large to be allowed to degenerate into a series of solo complaints, the priest made a valiant effort to link their comments with a text from *The Pilgrim's Progress,* reminding them that this book - one of the treasures of the English language in his opinion - had been written during the long years John Bunyan had been held, a prisoner of conscience, in Bedford jail. Brave Bunyan had suffered the pangs of hell in the bottomless pit. He'd been there. Done that. Bought the hair shirt. Three hundred years before. There was really nothing new in their experience.

The young man was moved to read out relevant snippets about the Slough of Despond; he offered pertinent lines concerning the life-styles of the Giant Despair of Doubting Castle, of Mr Fearing, of Mr Despondency and his daughter Miss Much-Afraid.

The Goths exchanged puzzled glances. Stella was quite certain they would have responded more readily to the stories of Mister Miserable and Little Miss Scaredy-Cat.

Lily was hearing not a word of this. She appeared completely detached from her surroundings, her mind elsewhere. Stella noticed that the girl's huge eyes had suddenly focussed in terror and disbelief on the third shadowy occupant of their pew. When she turned her head to see if the gaze was returned, Stella was alarmed to find that the man's glittering eyes were directed, not at Lily, but at herself. Caught staring, he looked away but swiftly back again and his head went up in defiance. With a rough gesture he tugged down the hood of his monk's habit and sneered. A scent of something woody and precious was released from the folds. The scent of an up-market embalming fluid, Stella thought with a shudder. Frankincense? At any rate, an expensive scent at odds with the brutal features the man now displayed. In the candle-light, his shaven head gleamed with the grey-blue colour of a corpse, the misshapen ear he turned to her sheltered the tattooed head of a snake whose coils reappeared to twine about his neck. Hideous but expertly done. Stella would have dismissed him as 'Designer Goth' had she not noticed the uncertain line of a broken nose which marred what could have been a handsome profile and indicated a studied carelessness about his appearance, as did the untreated wound in the lobe of his left ear from which an earring seemed to have been recently torn. Stella saw with disgust that it was still seeping blood.

Her training reminded her that earlobes bled profusely

and this one, being on the point of healing, must have been damaged less than an hour ago. This man had been fighting savagely, perhaps only minutes before.

She shuddered and forced back an impulse to grab Lily by the hand and run out.

She noticed that Lily had reached for the Bible that sat along with the prayer book on the ledge in front of her. She had opened it up towards the end and was pointing with some emphasis at the printed words. Stella followed the trembling finger and read from the first epistle of Saint Peter: ... *be vigilant, because your adversary, the Devil, as a roaring lion, walketh about, seeking whom he may devour.*

The finger underlined, once again, the word 'Devil' then lifted, turned through ninety degrees and pointed at the man with the ragged ear.

Stella calmed herself by mentally drawing up a prosaic police description of the accused. *Caucasian male, age: late twenties, estimated height: 6', dark complexion. Eye colour: flame. (They wouldn't believe that.) Distinguishing features... Where to start?*

She should have found him repellent but such was the power of his arrogant stare, she was losing herself in a hypnotised study of his face. His mouth twisted in mockery.

He knew who she was.

She cringed away from him as he leaned closer and murmured in her ear words which plunged an icicle of fear into her side: 'Tell her I'm waiting for her in the graveyard.'

At that moment the congregation grew weary of the Mister Men and especially scornful of Mr Valiant For Truth with his flashing sword and his heroics. They got up with relief at the priest's suggestion that they should reform into smaller discussion groups where everyone's voice might be heard and they began to mill about. Lily slipped quickly out of the pew, in an effort to avoid their companion, Stella guessed. By instinct she set off to follow Lily then turned to see if he was pursuing them. The man had vanished.

When she turned back, Lily too had disappeared. Stella hadn't been aware of the great door opening - the wretched girl must have put up her hood and lost herself in the crowd. She resigned herself to searching her way steadily through each group as soon as they'd all settled. She swiftly did this. No Lily.

She'd clearly made a dash for it but would have had to to pass through the churchyard where her Nemesis had declared he would be waiting. Judging that this was where the danger lay, Stella hurried to the door and pulled it open, panting with anxiety and openly calling Lily's name.

The churchyard was deserted and silent. The single lamp glowed uselessly in its corner, failing completely to penetrate the dense tuffets of evergreen shrubs. Stella crashed into the stillness, calling out, brambles tearing at her hands as she tried to plough her way through to the even thicker darkness at the back of the church. And a thought struck her, filling her with dismay. Didn't churches all have a second door - a vestry door? Was there a back way out of the church? One that she'd missed? A door straight into a killing ground?

Sobbing with fear, she heard heavy footsteps thudding after her and turned to see a large caped form striding towards her, arms outstretched. It seized her and clamped her arms to her sides.

'Get a grip, Constable! What the hell's going on?'

The wan lamp-light illuminated the granite features of Commander Loxley.

*

133

'Well, you don't think I'd let one of my officers go unsupervised into the mouth of hell, do you? Calm down, love, and have a swig of this.' He took a vacuum flask from an inside pocket of the antique police cape he was wearing and poured a measure into the cap. 'That'll buck you up. No harm, seeing as you're officially off-duty.' He peered at her as she sipped. 'Now listen - nobody got out of that church before you did. You're the first to leave.'

The strong coffee laced with brandy began at once to work its restorative magic. 'Sir, I must...'

'Don't worry, Sergeant Simpson is with me and I've left him on watch by the gate. Park your bum on that tombstone and tell me why you were crashing about through the undergrowth, whimpering, half way through the jollifications.'

He listened carefully to her report.

'Right. That's clear enough. And your friend with the serpent at his throat is not the Devil made flesh. He's known to us. Hang on a tick.'

He took out his mobile, dialled, spoke a few words and waited, a grin on his face. After a moment or two he passed her the screen. 'Here he is, they've patched it through for me. Recognise this charmer?'

Stella looked with distaste at the cocky, sneering face and nodded.

'Not Old Nick, perhaps, but next worst thing. Jules Lestrange he calls himself. Though he was Simon Sheppard before he graduated. Cambridge then Sandhurst. Ex-Guardsman. Ex for good reason: behaviour so reprehensible it turned the stomachs of his fellow officers and he was given the boot. And the Army's loss was our loss. He moved back to his alma mater. Keeps a second-hand bookshop a few yards from the church, down the snicket. Hobbies: Ancient History - he ponces about in a medieval monk's robe, he drives fast cars, purveys dodgy substances to undergraduates to pay for the wheels and beats up young girls. He preys on the weak and insecure: young, foreign, self-doubting... And we're not short of those in the city. The toe-rag's cleverer than your average copper and always one or two steps ahead of the Plod. Drugs and Vice would like to nail him.' The commander's face was grim. 'If your cousin's entangled with this piece of pond-life, she was right about needing a lifebelt all right. Still, at least she was still alive when she slipped through your fingers. Drink up and we'll go back and see if Simpson's seen anything.'

Sergeant Simpson had seen no one leave. No Lily. No Lestrange. They waited and watched. They passed around the flask.

The Goths turning out at the end of the meeting objected querulously to an inspection by flashlight and added police intimidation to their list of grievances but they went on their way towards the pizza parlour untroubled.

The church clock was striking eleven when the last of them drifted off. The priest locked up and came down the path to greet Loxley by name.

'Any luck, Commander?' he asked. 'Did you get him?'

'Nothing much to report,' Loxley replied carefully. 'Two of your customers in whom we have an interest seem to have done a runner.' And then, at the sight of Stella's agonised face: 'We'll go on looking through the night. Reverend, would you object if I sent a small crew in at first light to comb through this undergrowth? Just to be on the safe side. Leave no gravestone unturned and all that...' He accepted with grace the priest's eager offer to be present at the operation. 'This is the old graveyard, isn't it? Thought so. No, don't worry, I'll give instructions not to disturb any any sleeping Saxons.'

*

135

Stella's phone rang at eight, just as she was about to start for headquarters. She listened dully to the impersonal message which asked her to present herself as soon as possible at the crime scene at All Hallows' Church.

Crime scene? It hadn't been the scene of anything but imagined terror when she'd left it the night before.

The perimeter of the church premises was now outlined by a blue and white plastic police ribbon and Simpson's replacement was on duty at the gate, waiting for her. 'They're round the back,' he said. 'They think you can identify the body.'

*

She made her way through what remained of the undergrowth. Not so fearsome this morning. Parts of the graveyard appeared to have been given a comb-through and piles of foliage had been raked up in a corner allowing ancient grey headstones to surface into the half-light of the November morning. Round the back of the church she came upon an oddly assorted group of five. Two uniformed constables were taking directions from the Reverend Sweetman who was standing about, fresh in jogging gear, advising them on which fence post seemed the most easily removed to allow exit from the site into Peas Passage. An excited cry from the coppers announced that they'd found it. Her boss was talking to a suited police pathologist whom she recognised. Loxley looked tired and dejected and was still wearing his Victorian police cape. He'd been there all night. He gave her a shifty look and seemed reluctant to meet her eye when she joined them. He muttered something to the pathologist. Stella steeled herself for the worst possible sight.

She made out the grey-clad shape lying almost hidden behind a fallen gravestone and approached on leaden feet. Loxley drew back after a nod in her direction, leaving the formalities to the pathologist.

'Good morning Constable Kenton. Doctor Soames... Ian Soames.'

'I remember, sir. We've met before.'

The doctor moved closer and spoke softly: 'The inspector tells me you can confirm the identity of the deceased. We're pretty sure we know who this is but he insists that you take a look. But, Constable, there is a bit of a problem... a discrepancy... that will take some explaining. Would you mind?'

The corpse was lying on its back and someone had covered its face with a flap of the cloak. As Stella bent to examine it, Dr Soames gently pulled the cloak away from the features.

It was some time before Stella could bring herself to utter the words of identification. 'I believe this to be the man who calls himself Jules Lestrange. His career and details are known to Commander Loxley. I gave a description of him to the inspector. Last evening, after...'

Loxley was suddenly by her side with a warning hand on her shoulder. 'That'll do! Shush, lass! Don't say any more. There's something you ought to hear.'

Again Stella had the feeling the commander was writhing in discomfort. She looked back at the face of Lestrange and was herself struck with foreboding.

There was surely something wrong here?

She looked more closely at the candle-wax features of the dead man, his subdued corpse-colouring so faded that even the snake around his neck appeared long dead.

Loxley hissed in her ear: 'Stabbed to death. Three blows of a knife into his chest.'

His grip on her shoulder tightened, conveying a warning. 'But, Stella, the doc tells us he died at least three days ago.'

*

Stunned, she could barely take in the hurried professional conversation going on over the top of her head. 'Died here at the scene... blood loss... no weapon left behind... footprints... a trysting place?... Seems to have been.... certain... er... other evidence of illegal behaviour. And a path through the underbrush leading from the back door.'

While everyone else shuddered at the thought the doctor remarked: 'Odd people choose odd places for their odd activities. When they've exhausted natural thrills, they go for the supernatural. Gives a certain frisson. We're not young any more Commander, remember. Once upon a time....'He turned to direct a quizzical look at Stella. 'One thing we can be certain of is that he died here, *in situ*, and, I'm calculating, no later than last Tuesday.'

This was the point where she shouted: 'Stop! That's impossible! I saw this man in church only last night.'

And ruined her career for the sake of truth.

But the red-headed priest who'd been watching and listening had approached her silently. He smiled and spoke softly in her ear. 'May I recommend little Miss Valiant-For-Truth sheath her sword and zip her mouth? The monster's dead. Hang on to that! He did enough harm when he was alive. No need to give him the satisfaction of ruining three careers by his death. Your career, Loxley's and mine I mean. Let's take the stepping stones the Commander's about to offer us. We'll talk about this when we get to the other side.'

'We'll be needing your cousin's address, Kenton,' said Loxley.

He added quietly. 'If you were ever *on* the case - I'd say you were now *off* it. Go back to HQ and get on with your routine. There's no official record of your involvement. I'll make it my business to see to it that your name doesn't feature before, during or after the event.' He added in a kindly tone: 'I'll do what I can and I'll keep you informed.'

*

'We had to arrest and charge her, of course. But, in her favour, Lily did turn herself in. Murder weapon in one hand and victim's bloodied ear-ring in the other, who were we to argue? Full, if muddled, confession. Straightforward case of justifiable homicide. Medical evidence of abuse at his hands over some time. She'll get help rather than punishment.'

'But there's premeditation, sir! Lawyers can have a field day with that. The knife? She must have taken one with her to the church that Tuesday. That'll count against her.'

'No. They do flower arranging in the vestry, using six inch knives for what they call stem-splitting. The blades are fitted with natty green handles to show they're for gardening but anything that'll split a dahlia stem will sever an artery or pierce an aorta which this one did. In extreme distress, as he dragged her fighting out through the back, Lily snatched one up and killed him. Clear case of self-defence. Ran away in panic.'

'But why did she come back for the service on Friday night?'

'Having written a warning note to you earlier, she was counting on you turning up. She'd seen things were coming to a head, thought *she* would be the victim, and hoped you'd help. But disaster struck earlier than she'd calculated and she returned to the church to tell you what she'd done. She wanted to confess to someone who'd listen with sympathy.'

'But then she saw something nasty in the pew on Hallowe'en? Someone who shouldn't - someone who *couldn't* have been there?'

He stirred uneasily. 'Let's say that in her drugged state

she was spooked by something, shall we?' he said drily. 'Having a vision. She saw something very determined to make its evil presence felt. She lost courage and ran off by her usual route. Through the curtain they pull over the vestry door and out into the graveyard.'

'She went to check whether the body was still there. Perhaps she'd hallucinated about the whole thing and not actually killed him.'

He nodded. 'But what she found there terrified her even more. The body was still lying behind the gravestone where she'd dragged it. She ran out into Peas Passage. She hid herself away overnight then came in to tell the whole garbled tale next morning.'

'Poor little Lily! She must have been on drugs for quite a while?'

'Yes. We're fully accepting of that, of course. Detached from reality... no sense of time... hallucinations, as you suggest.... We made out her story eventually. With the help of forensics.'

'Ah, yes. Forensics. Death speaks for itself these days in clear scientific terms,' Stella murmured.

Loxley replied encouragingly: 'True. Can't argue with lab results. But - think on, lass! They eliminate the innocent and only finger the guilty and we should thank God for them.' And then he looked at her with understanding and added quietly: 'All the same... whoever's died... Death - it's always a dark issue, Constable.'

Cambridge Future

Sweet Alison

Cambridge, 2022.

'Coming! I'm coming! Just hold on a minute, will you?'

Before Tom could get his hands onto the locks, the voice rang out: 'Stand back!'

A locating thump was followed by a shattering blow. His door fell in and four officers brandishing nerve sprays and stun guns surged into his living room.

Gloved fingers twitching on buttons, eager to release an eye-searing spray or a body-blasting voltage, they surrounded him and held him skewered by the beams of their head-torches. Tom blinked watery old eyes and stood amongst them, shocked and defenceless and clutching his dressing gown about him.

'Morning, lads! Won't you come in?'

The voice was disconcertingly brisk and authoritative with an edge of humour and completely at odds with the elderly figure before them.

They hesitated.

A vital second or two that allowed Tom time to react. He'd been in more threatening situations. At least these goons spoke his language. Not the King's English exactly but the British police could still manage a few intelligible grunts. He smiled and held up both his hands in a gesture that said: 'Welcome' and 'I'm unarmed'.

The dressing gown fell open, revealing a sinewy old body dramatically criss-crossed with the tracery of healed wounds, gleaming silvery in the torchlight. He was wearing a pair of ancient union jack boxer shorts. One of the torches wobbled in reaction of some sort. Disgust? Hilarity? Tom noted the officer's number. Clearly this was the least experienced of these bully boys. It was the leader he needed to identify. One down, two more underlings to eliminate.

'So you couldn't sleep either?' he said genially. 'Early birds! 4 a.m.! I was just making a cup of tea. Fancy one?' With a gesture over his shoulder to the kitchen, he went on in a crisp officer's voice: 'Sit down, take the weight off. Won't be a minute. Kettle's just boiled.'

No one stopped him as he turned confidently and walked away. They let him get as far as the kitchen with its back door leading to the small garden, on to the back alleyway and out into the unlit, sleeping streets of Cambridge. The kitchen with its drawerful of well-kept knives and meat cleavers. While the kettle came back to the boil he tidied away the washing up and his fingers lingered on a 63 chef's knife. By the ancient rules of engagement, *they'd* chosen the venue, *his* was the choice of weapon. He smiled and slipped the knife back in the drawer. He'd made his choice. He needed to call on a resource more subtle than a sharp-edged blade.

They'd sent the B team. Not that there were any A teams left in the provinces. Real talent was drained away on Suburban Euroduty - Marseille or Athens or some other hell-hole or sent off to keep what passed for peace at the latest Middle-Eastern flash point. But this pack seemed to be armed, organised and acting on instructions. Better than attack dogs, and yet they had a weakness he could exploit. Tom began to gain confidence. He might just come through this if he could stay calm.

They were still standing about silently taking in the neat living room with its orderly bookshelves, good water-colours and painted dresser stacked with a cargo of blue and white china when he staggered back in with a tray of tea things and thrust it towards them with a wheeze and an apologetic smile.

The two officers who automatically put out hands to take the heavy tray from him were further discounted from Tom's list and he was left with the leader. The one who stood back and left the menial chores to his subordinates.

Take the leader out first. Thirty years ago number 8817 would have been the first to feel the side of Tom's hand smashing across his windpipe.

This morning the man was the target of no more than a smile and reassuringly mundane words: 'Hope you don't mind using these old Mister Men mugs? My grandchildren love them. Now – help yourselves... we've got Messrs Happy, Funny, Tickle and Mean. Pick whatever suits you.'

Tom smiled as three hands reached out and grabbed a mug, confirming his selection of leader who was left eyeing the remaining Mister Mean mug with derision. Tom handed it to him with no comment.

'Now then... Sugar? Digestive biscuit with that? I say - do tell your blokes to raise their visors. This is the very best Darjeeling. I'd like them to appreciate the colour.'

A nod from 8817 released three visors. Another slight victory. Tom liked to see his enemy's eyes.

They sipped their tea. 'Very nice, sir,' said the youngest – or Mister Happy as Tom now had him.

And – 'sir'? Another concession! He promised himself he'd get a 'sir' from the leader before he left. *Set an attainable goal. Attain it.*

'Oh, thank you. Glad you like it. Help yourself to a refill, won't you, Happy?'

'It's Josh, sir. Thanks. Don't mind if I do.'

'Nice to have company at this hour.' He addressed his remark to 8817. 'Mind telling me why you're here?'

The fourth visor clicked up. Not as a concession to him;

Tom deduced he was meant to be intimidated by the stony glare of the eyes as the mouth said sullenly: 'Do we really have to spell it out? Go on, let's hear you take a guess.'

'Never was fond of guesswork, officer. Sergeant, is it? Always prefer to work from facts, as I assume you do.' *Establish rapport.* 'Now, you'll be wanting to confirm my identity? If you'll allow me?'

He reached a wallet down from the mantelpiece, flipped it open and handed it over. 'Thomas Thorpe. Date of birth: 1957, age 65. Yup, I regret to say I've entered Life Stage Three. But no one threw a party!' No one laughed at his feeble joke either so he pressed on: 'Papers all in there. Tell me - wouldn't this seem just a bit like overkill? I mean - sending four fine young fellows like you to apprehend an old fart like me. And all for the purpose of conveying him a hundred yards down the road to the local sanctuary? I say, is this some sort of a training exercise?'

The eyes betrayed a sadistic enjoyment as 8817 delivered his next pronouncement. 'The Sanctuary? Is that what you thought we were here for? To give you a lift down the road to Geriatric Paradise? You should be so lucky! Naw! Think again!'

'Then I search my conscience and come up with no possible reason why you should have been sent here.'

'I'll give you one.' The sergeant waited for a tormenting moment before saying with relish and something more - perhaps a touch of surprise to hear himself actually pronouncing the word:'Murder.'

*

'Murder, eh?' Tom chose to echo the man's surprise. 'Sorry to hear that. Victim anyone I know?'

Oh, you know her all right. Ms Alison Swinton. Your Life Stage Three Advisor.'

'Alison Swinton? Good Lord!' Tom was visibly alarmed. His right arm began to tremble and he seized hold of it with his left to keep it steady. He shot a glance at the men to see if they had noticed the disability. They had. He struggled on: 'Alison? I have met the lady once but you're mistaken - she's not my personal advisor. Well, what about that, then! Poor little Alison! And murdered, you say? Tell me how she died.'

8817 opened his mouth and shut it again. He shuffled his feet. Finally: 'Not able to say. Yet.'

'Perhaps you're not aware, gentlemen... ?' Tom was perfectly sure they were aware and had accessed his bio-file before grabbing their spray guns and coming out. An armed squad would not have been sent to arrest or kill a run-of-the-mill Oldy. They must have been warned about his past: British Army Retired. Ex SAS. Terminal rank of Colonel. *Watch it, lads, the old goat's got form. May still be a bit frisky.*

'Oh, we're aware all right,' Mr Mean interrupted. 'Ms Swinton visited you here in your home a week ago. Last Tuesday the 25th of March at 3.15. on State business and she's not been seen since. Enquiries have been made and there are no sightings of her after her visit here and no e-coms from her either. End of the line: here. What have you done with her? Where is she, Thomas?'

'Colonel Thorpe, officer,' Tom corrected pleasantly. 'Bless me! What an extraordinary thing! And, yes, of course, I'll be pleased to help. You were quite right to come to me – I must have been one of the last people to see her. I know I was her last client that day – she said as much, I remember.' Tom hesitated. Telling the truth was always a dangerous game even with the aim of appearing open and honest. But he calculated they must have established this much already and he was merely reinforcing his innocence. 'However, gents, if I understand you correctly, this is a *disappearance* you're

146

investigating? You would seem to have no body? Do I have that right? So there's still hope she'll turn up? Is that what we're saying?'

'It's only a matter of time.' The sergeant strolled into the kitchen and flung the back door open. 'Bodies don't take long to surface.' His head torch swept the boundaries, illuminating rear wall, side fences and dwelling on the flower beds. 'Freshly dug,' he remarked. 'Now why am I not surprised to see that?'

Tom frowned. His voice was determinedly cheerful as he replied: 'Because it's Spring, of course! I never let myself get left behind by the seasons, sergeant. All prepared and ready for the bedding out next week. I've got salad crops going in... tomatoes... strawberries. All approved stuff. Can't do much heavy work any longer. He gestured briefly to his right arm. But with a trowel in my left hand and two eager grand-kids in harness, I get there. You'd see it's a bit hit and miss if you looked in the daylight,' he confided. 'But I like to encourage them. They'll get it right next year.'

The responding sneer said quite clearly: 'If there is a next year, you old fogey.'

The sergeant flicked open his communicator, established his link and spoke into it with deliberate clarity. 'Yeah, we're going to need that digging squad... Dog? Naw! Don't bother. It's only a few square feet. We can turn the whole lot over in a couple of hours.'

'I say, officer, it's early in the season, you know - not everything's showing yet. Your men won't know what to spare. Some of those plants are quite rare.'

'They'll be even rarer by the time the lads have finished.'

The dull black eyes were pitiless. With a feeling of physical sickness which he turned his head to conceal, Tom resigned himself to surrendering his garden. *Know when to abandon. Let go.*

He changed tack. 'Now let me think. Ms. Swinton

seemed perfectly well and normal when she left at 4 p.m. And she *did* leave! On her own two feet.' He turned back into the living room and shut the doors. His face clouded and he found himself explaining into the silence: 'Not a particularly happy interview for reasons I'm sure you'll understand.'

And that was putting it mildly, he thought, remembering. This was looking bad for him. He'd need to tread very carefully. All too easy to end up as a died-while-resisting-arrest statistic.

The death blow would come from the sergeant.

Tom was puzzled to be picking up a feeling of pent-up violence and even antipathy from the small portion of face visible between helmet and chin-strap. He discounted a personal element. This could only be a sample of the usual age-aversion. All Third Stagers were a drain on public resources, an embarrassment at the best, a menace to be eliminated at the worst.

One piece of rough handling and this crew would have cleared away two problems. Ticked two boxes in their action programmes. Ms Swinton's presumed death solved by a show of guilt - they might even claim: confession. And a reduction by one in the geriatric surplus figures. A good morning's work. They'd get a commendation, perhaps even a bonus.

Tom's strategy was simple: Get out of this alive.

His tactics, not so clear. The wretched woman's disappearance, coinciding, as it did, with her visit to him, was difficult to explain. He couldn't cruise through on the assumption that she would just turn up. And time and resources were stretched to the limit these days; no one was prepared to give anyone, particularly an Oldy, the benefit of the doubt. He reckoned that he had until the end of this interview to establish his innocence. Half-an- hour? That was the time-span they would have been allotted.

He had thirty minutes to prove his innocence of a crime they could not even know had been committed.

Time. Nothing more precious when it was running low. Time. One of the heroines of his childhood had known how to make the most of it. That ace story-teller, Sheherazade. Fascinating and intelligent woman - completely wasted on the murderous Persian king she'd married. But, by her skills, she'd kept his interest - and her head on her shoulders - not for just one night but for a thousand and one nights (Tom liked to add - at least) and the result was a collection of the world's most magical folk tales. He was working his way through them with his grandchildren. And he was determined to finish. He needed three more years. He'd be content with that.

He decided on his tactics. Operation Sheherazade. He'd hit them with it.

'Murdered, eh? Well, are we surprised? Honestly? You might say she had it coming, don't you think?'

They looked at him blankly. One of them growled a warning.

'Sit down, lads. I have things to tell you about Ms Swinton that are decidedly off the record. Rather surprising things. I'm assuming you know her hair was not naturally blonde? That she bites her fingernails? Thought so! Trivialities. Well - the information I have is much more discreet and personal.' His voice took on an involving and titillating animation. 'Info that could well explain her disappearance.'

'Before you go any further, Thorpe, may I remind you that you are speaking of a lady who is... was... our co-worker?' complained the leader petulantly. 'The Stage Three Advisory Bureau depends on the co-operation of the Social Enforcement Division. That's us. We've all worked closely with Ms Swinton in the past and don't care to hear your defamatory comments.'

Tom was pleased to hear the note of personal interest

being shown at last. Pleased also to watch them, at a gesture from him, taking up his invitation to sit themselves around his coffee table.

So, he'd got it! They were angered by the suspicion that he'd done damage to one of their own. Solidarity of the Unit. A strong motivation. He'd respect it. And use it. He had about forty more years experience of unit solidarity than these fellers. But he also knew the value of inter-unit intrigue and gossip.

'Sergeant, I hope I am never less than courteous, especially where a lady is concerned. Rather old-school you'll find me, in that regard, I fear. But if it becomes necessary to speak an uncomfortable truth or two in the interests of solving a crime, you may count on my full co-operation. And uncomfortable truths is what we're looking at, I'm sorry to say. Secrets! Scandals! Ms Swinton was not, perhaps, exactly the woman you thought she was!'

Four helmets leaned forward by a telling centimetre. He had their interest.

'Oh, an efficient officer, well trained, correct.' They nodded agreement with the sentiment. (Brainwashed, pre-programmed tool of the State on whom the usual heart and brain lobotomy had been performed, was Tom's private opinion.) 'She'd come to check my level of physical and mental capability, examine my residency permit. You know the sort of thing.'

'To advise you it was time to move on? To the Chestnuts?' The voice was impatient. The sergeant looked around the room. 'Nice little house. But wasted on one person. Could take a unit of four, no bother. How've you managed to swing it?'

'Staying on in my own house, all bought and paid for years ago?' Tom stifled the sudden flare of rage in his tone as he went on: 'Special dispensation. It's all there signed and stamped and on file. It helps to have friends

in high places, sergeant. And I mean: very high places!'
he lied. He tapped the side of his nose in an age-old
gesture of cunning. 'Know what I mean?'

Stony silence as they digested this. Like all
functionaries, they were impressed by higher authority
as much as they resented it. The mantel clock struck the
quarter hour. Tom dashed on.

'Daughter-in-law works for the government.
Agricultural scientist. In seed development. So hush-
hush even her husband doesn't know what she gets up
to! He's a pilot in the Presidential Eurofleet.'

He gave them time to take this in. The one or two
airlines the world's resources supported these days were
only at the disposal of the rich, the powerful and state
functionaries. Piloting one of their planes was a much
sought-after way for an ordinary bloke to see the world.
That his son had secured such a job would impress these
macho types in front of him if nothing else would.

'So - I was granted special permission to act as child-
carer-by-kinship until such time as I keel over or they
reach fourteen. Jack and Polly spend half their time with
me. Occasionally here, mostly over at their place in
Melton. I'm not authorised for a car so I get the guided
bus or I'm picked up by one or other of their parents,
according to their schedules. My daughter-in-law never
knows where or when the Minister is going to need her
to go next. Not a perfect life, sure you'll agree, but we all
have to make do and manage these days, don't we?'

The sergeant referred to notes on his palm screen.
'Inessential, unjustifiable and uneconomic
arrangement.'

'Exactly the words Alison used.' Tom made it sound
like a compliment on their acuity. 'But, gentlemen, why
don't you hear for yourselves how the interview went?'

They looked on in puzzlement as he took a small device
from a drawer. 'Don't mock,' he warned them. 'I know it's

twenty years old but it still works a treat! We used to call these voice recorders. You can still get the batteries on Dump-IT. I usually record interviews. You never know when you'll need to use it in evidence.' He tried to play down any suggestion of triumph as he added: 'And here she comes - the lady introduces herself.'

'Stage Three Advisory Bureau, Miz Alison Swinton.' The remembered and hated voice grated.

And Tom cringed to hear himself replying with a nervous attempt at humour: 'STAB operative after me, eh? I'll be careful not to turn my back on you then! Ha! Ha!'

'That's what they all say,' Mister Funny drawled wearily.

Tom's voice again, asking pleasantly: 'You don't mind if I record our little chat, do you?'

'If you really feel you must,' Ms Swinton sighed in irritation.

Tom remembered clearly her truculent face. What could have been handsome features on anyone with a sense of humour or a kind disposition were twisted into a gargoyle mask of suspicion, aggression and scorn. The fluffy blonde hair-cut was too young for her and at odds with the hard grey eyes, the deep red lips, the narrow nose.

'Such a pretty girl,' he commented.

They all grunted in agreement.

Alison Swinton's flat voice chuntered on as he restarted the tape and passed the machine to the sergeant. 'Here, help yourself.'

'Lovely home, Thomas. Family of four easily... wasteful arrangement... sure we can think of something... place will become available at the Chestnuts just down the road in - oh, shall we say, a fortnight?'

The sergeant fiddled with the fast-forward button and flipped through the ensuing passage of protest from Tom, the rustle of forms he presented for inspection and played the next passage that caught his interest.

'It's the issue of the water consumption we must address, Thomas. We are in possession of the Water Company figures, you see. It has come to our notice that you are using much less than might be expected.'

'*Less*? Not quite sure what you have to complain about then.'

'In cases like these, we always find that a downward trend in water consumption is a sure indication that our Advisee has deteriorated physically. Plunged into a vicious circle of self neglect. No washing, Thomas. Of body, clothes, fabric of home. Time to move on.'

And the angry response: 'But of course I use less water! I told you! I spend more than half my time baby-sitting away from home. In Melton. I'm a good citizen! Make do and mend, Save don't spend and all that rot! I obey all the ecological rules and then some! When I've seen to the children's baths - never more than four inches - I use the same water. And then I bale it out for the flower pots.' And, with a sudden loss of temper that made the squad jump: 'God, woman! I've survived in the desert for weeks on end! I think I know how to use water efficiently! It doesn't mean I've gone ga-ga! This is just a trumped-up excuse. Something to fit into a box on a form!'

A heated and repetitive exchange followed:

'Don't give me all that Eskimos on ice floes stuff! Pleeese! Don't you think I haven't heard it a hundred times? You Oldies can be so boooring!'

'State jackboots! Lobotomised jobsworths!'

Tom winced. He'd forgotten just how far he'd gone. He was alarmed by the look of triumph on the sergeant's face. But before he could accuse Tom of a rush of murderous rage, the ring of Ms Swinton's communicator sounded on the tape. The one she kept in her bag, not the official STAB one she'd placed on the table.

'Excuse me if I take this...' Without waiting for a reply,

she began to speak, her voice descending disconcertingly into a seductive purr. 'Oh, hi there, darling! No, don't worry, there's no one here. We can talk.'

Tom was to be heard distantly, clearing his throat and clinking china mugs on the dresser. 'I'll just pour out some coffee while you're otherwise occupied, Alison.'

'She set up her video and took the call right there where you're sitting, sergeant,' Tom explained. 'It seemed personal so I bustled off into the kitchen while she did it.'

'But, Bunnikins, you told me you'd get it organised! What are you saying - you *have*? Where? Majorca? Majorca! Bloody hell! I said Minorca! Course it bloody well makes a difference! But I'd set my heart on that hotel my sister went to... I told you! We'd agreed!'

At this point there was a click. 'That's Ms. Swinton turning the recorder off herself. While she continued her discussion with... hmmm...'

'With?' the sergeant asked. 'What are you suggesting?'

'That the lucky fellow traveller to Min or Maj-orca was not Mr Swinton!'

'What do you mean?'

'Our Ms was clearly Mrs. She wore a wedding ring. In the general exchange of pleasantries when she arrived I established that she'd been married for eight years. I showed her a photo of my wife though she wasn't really interested. Believe me, sergeant, the man she had at the other end - her Bunnikins - was not her husband of eight years! You can tell by the voice and I could see by the way she was prinking into the lens that she was all flirty with him. Until he fouled up in the matter of geography that is. I decided to do something quite mischievous. If you go on playing, you'll hear me come in again. I walked round behind her, sneakily switched on the recorder again, put a friendly hand on her left shoulder showing off my Rolex watch - old but good - to amaze and impress

154

Bunnikins, reached over and placed a cup of coffee in front of her.'

'No! I told you - it's no one! I'm on a house-call to an elderly client. We've got this old coot refusing to wash himself,' Ms Swinton was heard protesting.

'It was one of those Wedgwood cups on the dresser. If you should ever trace this vid-e-com, sergeant, you'll see it happen just as I said. Those cups are very recognisable,' Tom offered eagerly.

He guessed from the swift averting of the eyes and the failure to follow up with a question that the sergeant had, indeed, had access to this call. They'd seen the evidence already. And they must have identified the mystery man at the other end by now.

'Ah! You've done your homework. You've traced him? Great! Let me think... Private call, not departmental... You'd have needed to get hold of her own phone. Did she leave it in her car? She came in a car.'

'How would you know that? There's no parking in this street.'

'She was wearing very high spiky heels and a tight skirt. It would have killed her to walk a hundred yards in that get up.' He grinned. 'And - all right - I'll come clean - I actually saw her put her keys down on the table when she sat down. She must have parked her car along the Piece... No? Well, down the Cat and Moon Alley, then?'

Tom glanced at his clock. Six minutes to go.

'So. You did the sensible thing and worked through the CCTV footage until you picked up her car in Cat and Moon Alley.' Tom knew perfectly well that the CCTV cameras down there, all old swivel-and-shoot ones, were not in working order and hadn't been for six weeks. He'd heard the landlord at the Cat complaining about it. No one had bothered to install cameras, let alone keep them serviced, on Tom's own quiet street since cars, even the little electric bugs, were banned in the centre. Satellite surveillance was only available in politically sensitive areas like the capital, not wasted in peaceful towns like Cambridge. It must have presented them with something of a problem. Tom chortled silently as he calculated that they'd had to get off their arses and do their enquiring the old-fashioned way - on their feet, banging on doors.

'That's right. We got it up on CCTV.' The sergeant went for the easy lie. 'Her car's been retrieved. It was still there right where she'd parked it. Not vandalised luckily. The phone was under the front seat out of sight.'

'Well that's a start,' said Tom happily. 'SOCOs will be able to find all sorts of stuff in there! Possibly physical evidence of the precise nature of the relationship with the mystery caller? It's looking to me as though we've got two strong leads here in the enquiry: her husband and her lover. In fact: the usual suspects! Start of any Greek tragedy!' He was beginning to enjoy himself and wondered at the coppers' lack of enthusiasm for the chase. She's probably holed up in some little love-nest somewhere continental, using up three years' travel allowance in one go! Let's hope the chap's worth it! What do you say, Josh?'

Alarmed to be so addressed, the young copper stammered out a response: 'Er... sounds very likely to me, sir.'

'Scott? What are your thoughts?' Tom invited, smiling eagerly at the sergeant. He looked like a Scott.

'That's Peter,' the man corrected automatically and - Tom thought - surprisingly.

'Sorry, Peter. Well?'

'Yup. Don't think you're the first or the only one to have that idea. We're already following up this line of enquiry. But the fact remains that this house is the last location we have for her and we've not got to the bottom of your involvement yet. Tempers raised on both sides it seems to me. A man with your record. Desert Storm was it?'

Tom nodded. 'Thirty years ago. December 1990. When we still had a British Army. Before you were out of nappies, Peter,' he added flatteringly. His secretive division didn't hunt their fox by day and they never discussed their exploits with anyone. But they were allowed to lie in order to spread confusion. Oh, yes, they could lie. 'A month before the Storm broke, it was! By Land Rover through the Arabian Desert, behind enemy lines, travelling by night, tracking down and neutralising Saddam's SCUD missiles. And their operatives. In their fortified bunkers. Bit of a scramble, I'm afraid. Their troops were thicker on the ground than anyone had envisaged. I got myself torn up a bit doing roly-polys through three thicknesses of barbed wire.' Tom grinned. 'But we didn't lose a single bloke.'

'Trained to kill with bare hands, I understand. How many men have you killed, then, Colonel?' the sergeant asked.

Good Lord! The man genuinely wanted to know, Tom realised with a sick lurch. *An advantage shows itself - exploit it.* 'I remember every one, Peter,' he replied calmly. 'Close quarters work mostly. You never forget the look in a man's eyes, his eyes holding yours as you sink the blade into a soft place... Pleading... hating... defying... but, in the end, glazing over.' Reciting this garbage was making his gorge rise. He made a dismissive gesture and hurried on: 'Killing never gets easy; it never gets routine. I've accounted for thirty-five,' he improvised with quiet defiance. 'Hand to hand.'

They all let out whistling breaths.

'And all male?' the sergeant asked, carefully.

'That's right, Peter. All killed in the heat of battle.'

Three minutes left. Sheherazade would have moved on to the cliff-hanger by now.

'Look, why don't you just press the button and play the last bit? There's something you really ought to hear.'

The sergeant obliged.

The heated argument was resumed, the change in the woman's voice chilling. It was clear that she was quite deliberately going about the business of working him up to a show of temper. An unprofessional shouting match ensued and Tom shuffled awkwardly, uncomfortable to be overheard bargaining and begging. Finally, with a screech, Ms Swinton announced that she was leaving for now but the minute she got back to headquarters she'd organise a squad that would be less accommodating to his views. She'd have him out of his cosy little slot within the day. 'Better go and pack a washbag,' she finished nastily.

The machine played the sound of her heels clicking over the floorboards, the wrenching open of the door. Tom's bleating, automatic courtesy: 'Here, let me do that...' and the final rasping, 'Goodbye you old twit! You'll be hearing from us!' And the door banged loudly. After a long moment when the only sounds were of Tom blowing his nose into a handkerchief and sniffling, there came one last sigh and the machine was switched off. The sergeant carefully let it play on for a few more seconds to make sure he'd missed nothing but they heard only the hissing of the tape.

*

It was Josh who broke the silence. 'That's it? She just walked away? Like you said?'

'She did,' Tom confirmed.

Strangely, all four men slumped. The thought came to Tom that the buggers had genuinely suspected he was guilty of doing away with the woman all along. He hadn't been picked out of a hat as a token target. And here they were, disappointed, and no nearer coming up with a solution to their problem. Or were they?

'Er... this boy friend?' the sergeant asked, easing his meaty buttocks on his seat. For the first time, Tom recognised that the sergeant could have been thought attractive by some - in a D.H. Lawrence hero sort of way. 'Any idea of his name? Did she say a name? I didn't catch one on the tape.' He waited for an answer, eyes boring into Tom's.

The warning came from young Josh. An inadvertent narrowing of the eyes. The lad was suddenly very interested in the shiny caps of his boots.

'Careful, Tom!' he told himself. 'Something going on here... You could wreck it all with your next answer.'

He considered for a moment. 'No. Just slushy stuff. Kinder not to listen. Perhaps in the time she had it switched off?' He shrugged. 'No, sorry I can't help you there.'

As the clock struck the half hour, the four men rose to their feet.

'Well, thank you for your hospitality,' grunted the sergeant in a formal leave-taking. 'There's probably an explanation for all this. But that'll be all for the moment. You'll be hearing from us. Diggers'll be in to attend to the garden come daylight. Mustn't leave any stone unturned, must we? You'll thank us in the end, sir.' He sounded almost conciliatory.

Tom acknowledged the 'sir' with a nod. 'Oh, well...' He shrugged his shoulders. 'I dare say it could do with a good double-spit dig.' *Job done. Bear no rancour.*

*

As a slash of pink lit the sky from the east, he looked his last on the carefully tended oasis he'd created to keep the bleak world at bay. Would they spare the jasmine?

159

The mock orange? He longed to smell their old-fashioned perfume one last may-time. He'd take cuttings of them over for his son's garden, just in case. Growing things, sowing seeds: that was all that was left to him.

Quietly, over the years, Tom had been sowing other seeds with his grandchildren. Seeds of hope for humanity, delight in knowledge, the duty to identify a tyrannical authority and overturn it. They were enjoying classical history and philosophy. And, just in case, he was teaching them all he knew of unarmed combat. And survival.

That poisonous Swinton woman had threatened to cut his sowing time short.

He didn't care much for his own future - he'd lived enough to fill several life-times and he didn't in the least mind dying but while there were still vital things, life-affirming qualities, rebellious thoughts to be passed on, he would not be filed away in an ante-room to death. No Chestnuts for him as long as he had the wits and the strength to avoid it.

Tom watched the light grow stronger. The crew when they arrived, with or without dogs, would find nothing sinister in his patch. Waste of time. And an insulting underestimation of his intelligence. They'd be done by lunch time he reckoned. Better be - he was being picked up by his daughter-in-law for a sitting session. He'd gather up the trays of bedding plants and take them over to Melton. Spend the afternoon planting them. An investment in the future. The only kind possible for him in this uncongenial land he'd fought for but no longer recognised. The kids could help when they got out of school.

It was as he went to gather up the used coffee cups that it occurred to him. He almost dropped the tray in shock.

The sergeant had been sitting exactly where Ms.

Swinton had parked herself. Tom remembered the last question the man had asked him: 'Did you hear the boy friend's name mentioned?' He recalled the youngest copper's off-key reaction. He belatedly remembered that the sergeant had already seen the private conversation recorded by Swinton's communicator. He must already have known that she had indeed let slip an endearment or two. Possibly even a name when Tom had been in the kitchen. He'd asked the question, not to come up with a name - he didn't need to - he wanted to be sure that *Tom* was unaware of it. Tom felt weak with relief that his responses had been uncommittal.

Bunnikins... Rabbit... Peter Rabbit... Peter. Blimey! Could it be? Tom didn't know whether to laugh or cry. What had the poor dope said? 'Our two departments work closely together.' In more ways than one, apparently. Tom sat down, his mind racing, trying to work out the implications. The other men seemed aware of the relationship. Did they suspect their dark-eyed thug of a sergeant capable of murder? Having failed to pin the disappearance on Tom, perhaps they were even now trying to force a confession of some sort from the luckless husband? Tom grinned. Wherever they assigned the blame, it would be filed away in the end as an unsolved domestic. The police involvement would make it a case to be handled with what passed for discretion these days. They'd established that Tom was himself an innocent witness but not in any way a witness who could point the finger at one of their number. They'd checked him out and found him harmless. He relaxed. He'd have another cup of tea to celebrate his new day and he'd really enjoy this one.

He put his recorder away in the drawer, still smiling.

He hadn't bothered to switch it back on again last Tuesday, when, one minute after the door had banged shut behind her, he'd heard the knock. He'd left the door on the latch and she barged straight back in again, red in the face with fury. 'Forgot my keys,' she rasped. 'I think I left them on the table.'

'Ah, come in, do. I thought you'd be back. You see, you didn't forget them. I picked them up and put them in my pocket.'

'You did what? The hell with you! Why would you do that, you meddling old tosser?'

She advanced a few steps, inquisitive eyes narrowing. 'And what's that stuff you're messing about with? Plastic bags? They've been phased out! You're not supposed to have those! And rubber gloves? They're professionals-only issue. Just how many environment laws do you break in one day, Thomas?'

'I always thought the bags would come in handy. We used to use them for dumping rubbish, you know. I nicked the gloves on my induction visit to the Chestnuts. And I kept your keys because I shall need to drive your car tonight. When it gets dark. Two seater, is it? Good. Parked it in the Cat and Moon Alley I think you said?'

'I can have you arrested for this!' Triumph was followed straight away by dawning suspicion. 'What are you playing at?'

'Not playing, Ms Swinton. I don't play games.' He smiled sadly. 'In fact you might say I'm in deadly earnest.'

He'd held out the keys and jangled them, tormenting her.

Alison Swinton, with a howl of rage, dashed across the room to snatch them from his fingers. Straight into his lethal orbit. He'd spun her round at the last moment and broken her neck from behind with his strong right hand. He couldn't look into her eyes. Must be getting old.

*

162

The hairs on the back of Tom's neck warned him of the stealthy approach as he knelt, working on the new flower bed he'd dug, way out beyond the shrubbery in his son's garden. He heard a thrush call and fall abruptly silent. He tensed, all senses alert, but kept on digging until the stalker got within six feet of him.

He leapt up, turned, grabbed the little girl and swung her around his head. 'Gotcha! Hi there, Miss! You're useless! Noisier than a tap-dancing elephant. Where's that brother of yours?'

A stick poked sharply into the small of his back. 'Right behind you! We got you grandpa!' The boy jabbed at him again, crowing with delight. 'There! Right in the kidneys! *Stage a diversion.* We tracked you down by the wheelbarrow marks across the grass. What are you doing over here? Cor, you've done a lot of digging! You're a really useful engine, Thomas!'

Eager to join him in his activity, they settled to see what he was busy with. Tom explained the thought behind the new flower bed. Old English flowers were fast becoming extinct in gardens, going the way of the butterfly and the honey bee, he reported. Only vegetables and fruit were acceptable to the government these days. It was better placed where he'd put it, right out of sight of the house. If the SatSpy picked it up they could say it was a herb garden. That might pass. It could be a secret for the three of them. Well, they could tell their Mum too. She'd understand what grandpa was up to. The flowers of his youth with the wondrous scents and evocative names were dying out. Here was their chance to save a bit of history. He pointed to the four or five species of bedding plant he'd scavenged and put together, teaching their names and habits. He told them how to collect the seed come autumn and store it for another year. Their mother would help them if he wasn't around. She'd know what to do.

'What's this white one, grandpa? You've got a lot of that,' Polly noticed.

'Ah yes. Quite pretty isn't it? But it has a strange scent. I always think it smells a bit rank... a bit foxy. Have a sniff. It used to smell even worse until they bred this sweeter-smelling version. It's *Alyssum Odoratum.* Sweet Alyssum.'

'Sweet Alison, did you say, grandpa?'

'That's right. That's another word for it. "Sweet Alison" will do very nicely. It should grow well here. And I think we'll put some of this blue Forget-Me-Not right next to it.'

Lightning Source UK Ltd.
Milton Keynes UK
UKOW06f0254281015

261489UK00001B/69/P